# THE BODY ON THE ROOF

## KEVIN CREAGER

Black Rose Writing | Texas

ISBN: 978-1-68433-271-7
PUBLISHED BY BLACK ROSE WRITING
www.blackrosewriting.com

Printed in the United States of America
Suggested Retail Price (SRP) $17.95

*The Body on the Roof* is printed in Calluna

This book is dedicated to my wife, Sue, who has always believed that I was full of stories just waiting to come out, and to my children – Colin, Alex, and Laura – who quickly learned I was good at making up stories to answer all their questions.

# ACKNOWLEDGEMENTS

I wish to thank the many readers that I badgered into reading the initial drafts, in particular, my father, Charles Creager, and Mrs. Cheryl Lowe's fifth-grade language arts class of Mills Lawn Elementary School in Yellow Springs, Ohio. They provided immeasurable feedback and the encouragement to continue. I also wish to thank Michael Giorgio, of the AllWriters' Workplace and Workshop, for his coaching and insights, and Carl Ahlm, for his final editing.

# THE BODY ON THE ROOF

# CAST OF CHARACTERS

## PROLOGUE

Martin "Bud" Addams – current Police Chief of Summerfield, Ohio

Carl Ulicny – Hollywood movie producer and decider of Summerfield's fate

Betty Blockinger – Mr. Ulicny's secretary and the door to the great man

## CHAPTER 1 AND SO ON...

Jeff Pierson – Police Chief of Summerfield, Ohio

Marie "Hazy" Hazlett – civilian employee of Summerfield Police Department

Stephanie "Speed" Reasoner – police officer – nominally second in command

Martin "Bud" Addams – most junior police officer

George "Pops" Peabody – most senior police officer

Grace Mathison – widowed, retired school teacher

Dr. Peter Ross – Coroner/local physician – sees bodies coming and going

Phil Culbertson – Crime Scene Investigator

Mel Johnson – insurance agent for Johnson & Johnson Insurance Company – sometime companion of Grace Mathison

Harry Townsend – recently-hired insurance agent for Johnson & Johnson – nephew of Grace Mathison

Sherri Northrup – receptionist for Johnson & Johnson – any news in town primarily travels through Sherri

Julius "Big Mac" MacIntyre – co-owner of Mac's Café – don't tell anyone his real name is Julius

Jonathan John "JJ" Plummer – Mayor of Summerfield and attorney specializing in paperwork

Matt Laurenfeld – the local attorney that gets called on for court cases

Hazel Bucholtz – neighbor of Grace Mathison – former elementary school principal – nothing gets by her

Judy Pierson – wife of Jeff Pierson

JoAnn Pierson – excitable daughter of Jeff and Judy Pierson

Hank Peters – owner of Peters Hardware

Mike Wannamaker – former chief of police – still available for light duty

Larabeth Nelson – member of The Summerfield Literary Society

Nellie Chamberlain – member of the Summerfield Literary Society and maker of award-winning cheesecakes

Mindy Rhodes – member of The Summerfield Literary Society

Susan Peabody – member of The Summerfield Literary Society and long-suffering wife of George Peabody

Charlene Matthews – manager of the Summerfield Bank

Sharon Alvarez – Lincoln County District Attorney

Sam (or Seth) Getty – recently graduated from the police academy – had been filling in for the Oldstown Police Department

Seth (or Sam) Getty – recently graduated from the police academy – had been filling in for...well you know the rest

Emmett Doolittle – does the yard work for the Mathison property, whether it needs it or not

Gail Whittier – Assistant District Attorney, the only one that matters to Officer Addams

Luellen McMahon – dog-walking witness

Fifirello – Mrs. McMahon-walking witness, but she's not talking

Tracy Skinner – daughter of Cecil Skinner, lover of ice cream

# PROLOGUE
## (As close to present day as we can get)

Martin Addams was not looking for money, or fame, or even recognition.

All he wanted was to make sure that somebody, somewhere, knew what had actually happened, or, at least, as much as he knew about what really happened.

At the moment Addams was in the perpetually sunny state of California, sitting in the waiting room of the well-known movie producer, Carl Ulicny. He had been waiting there for some time. The appointment had been for 9:00, but it was now 9:42. That may not seem like a long time in the big city of Los Angeles, but, in his hometown of Summerfield, Ohio, you had better have a good reason for keeping someone waiting that long. And it had better be a particularly good reason.

The receptionist picked up the phone on her desk, though Addams could have sworn it hadn't rung. According to the nameplate on her desk, she was a Miss Blockinger. She listened for a moment then put the receiver back down.

"Mr. Ulicny will see you now, Mr....Addams."

After sitting for so long, it took some effort to get back up. Addams was a middle-aged, slightly overweight, slightly uncoordinated African-American, but he hadn't grown up as an African-American (or middle-aged or overweight). He'd grown up as Black, because that was the appropriate term at the time. He would just as soon that there wasn't any label involved at all. But he was aware that there were people that were always going to think of him as Black or African-American, just as there were always going to be people that thought of him as fat or clumsy. They were going to pick whatever adjective fit their need at the moment. He finally managed to rise and went through the indicated door.

He was currently police chief of Summerfield, a small Midwestern town with Midwestern values, whatever that meant to politicians and 24-hour news channels, and had been asked to come in to meet with this Carl Ulicny about a movie based on a book. A book that told the story of one of the strangest cases the town and the police department had ever encountered. It happened thirty years ago early in his career, but he was now the only one who had been actively involved that was in a position to act as a consultant. The only one still on duty, so to speak.

Basically, the book told the facts of the story accurately. He had to give Paul Cousins, the author, and former editor of *The Summerfield Weekly*, credit for that. Now he wanted to make sure the movie was going to keep getting it right.

"Good morning, Chief Addams. Good to meet you and glad to see you could make it so early." Ulicny, probably as old as Addams, but with less hair and a more expensive suit, pointed to a seat, another deep leather chair that was going to be even harder to get out of.

"You can call me 'Bud', everybody else does. Summerfield is not a big enough town to be 'Chief' all the time."

"Good, good. Glad to hear it. If this picture goes as well as I think it will, then you can call me 'George'. If it doesn't, then just don't call me." He chuckled. "A little Hollywood joke."

"Oh." Addams tried to smile.

Ulicny took his own seat. "Now, I really like this book. Really like it. Love it, in fact. I think it will be a great movie. We're going to have to jazz it up a bit, add some spice; you know how movies are. But, and I hope you appreciate this, I do want to keep it as accurate as possible. Keep the basic story. You know, 'based on a true story', as they say. So that's why I asked you to come in."

Addams nodded as if he actually understood what Ulicny wanted.

Ulicny continued. "Now I understand you were there, were on the scene. Were you police chief then, too?"

"Oh no. I'd only been there a little less than a year. I was the youngest member of the department."

"But you worked hard and became chief, huh? A 'rise-to-the-top' story, hey?"

"Yeah, sort of ..." Addams wondered if Ulicny had actually read the book at all. But the question got him thinking back.

Initially, it had never entered his mind to aspire to be police chief. When he was a brand-new officer, he had been in decent shape, enough to run around a tennis court once a week, even if he wasn't any good at it. And his overall awkwardness was never on public display – his friend, Roy, merely needed someone as a target for the tennis ball. Now being chief physically involved sitting in a lot of meetings, and doing a lot of paperwork, and simply being available. That didn't help keep him in shape. And, now, if he fumbled something, it was in front of a group of people who expected more from him.

When he had become chief, it had seemed to be the only sensible option at the time, at least to the town council. But he had worked hard and had built up what he hoped was a good reputation in town. And reputation was important in Summerfield. Very, very important.

# CHAPTER 1
## Summerfield, Ohio
### (Thirty-some years ago – give or take a lifetime)

The call came in just after eight in the morning. A wet, dreary morning following a major thunderstorm that lasted most of the night. Still overcast, still dripping, a good morning to do paperwork. For somebody, maybe, but not for Jeff Pierson, the chief of police for Summerfield. Pierson was in his early forties and still in what could be considered good physical condition, but mornings, and particularly wet mornings made it hard to get motivated.

A body had been found. What that meant heaven only knew, but Pierson knew he was the one that needed to find out. When first given the address, he immediately recognized it and quietly asked, "Mrs. Mathison?". Marie Hazlett, the dispatcher, grimaced and shrugged with an equally soft, "Could be, but that's all I got – a body on a roof."

"Well, she's a widow. Wouldn't think there'd be anybody else's body on her roof." He sighed.

The police department consisted of Hazlett's desk behind a counter facing the main door, an open area behind her with a small table and four two-walled open cubicles, three of them assigned to current officers, and the fourth waiting for an increased budget, but its desk currently stacked with files. Pierson's small, enclosed office was to the left of that main door and along the wall beyond that was another door connecting the department to the rest of city hall, and then two rooms, built as conference or interview areas. A last door at the end of the open area led to a hallway with a small kitchen, restroom facilities, a storage/evidence room, and three empty cells intended for strictly temporary usage.

Pierson shrugged into his jacket and headed out a back door for the squad car parked behind the police station. The police station was set in the right half of city hall and faced the southwest end of the central village green. All of the downtown businesses circled the park with its bandstand, trees, and grassy areas. Coming out of the parking lot and turning left to head north around the green, he had no difficulties in figuring out where to go. He, as well as most of the rest of the force, had been there before. Mrs. Mathison's was toward the edge of town, but it didn't take him long to get to her home – everything in Summerfield was within fifteen minutes of everything else, at rush hour. And rush hour was gone. The school buses were done with their morning routes, the shops weren't going to open for another hour or two, and people were already at their eight o'clock jobs, so traffic was light. Ten minutes. Maybe.

North of the green, he passed the Summerfield Church of Hope and Light on his right, then the Kramer Elementary School. He hoped everyone was already in class because he was well above the school speed limit. This end of town was primarily residential, with no lights or stop signs on the main street, so he pulled up in front of the Mathison home in just eight minutes.

Two of his officers were already there, Stephanie Reasoner, his nominal second-in-command, and Martin Addams, still considered a rookie, though he had been with them nearly a year. Neighbors were starting to gather, and drapes were drawn open across the street to stare at the law as there wasn't much of anything else to look at yet. It was still too early for all the houses to be awake, but two men with jogging outfits were talking to Addams.

As Pierson rose from the car, zipping up his jacket, Reasoner, trim and with the energy of the late twenties, moved toward him. He peered at the gray sky, still slightly leaking. "A might cold and damp out here. Morning, Speed." Pierson had nicknames for everyone. Reasoner ran track in college and was probably, no, certainly, still the fastest in his department.

"Morning, Chief." If his officers had nicknames for him, they made sure he didn't hear them.

"What do we have here? Hazy just said a body on a roof."

"Come over here to this corner. You can't see it from the street because of the overhanging tree branches. Tim Woods and Hal Pushkinz, there with Bud, were out running this morning and glimpsed it only from the angle two houses down. They had to come closer to the house before they could tell it was really something. It's a body."

"That's what I've heard."

They sloshed across the sodden lawn to the west corner of the house. She pointed up, and now he could see the body on the roof. Or what they could actually see was the bottom half of a body, wedged behind a heating vent half hidden under some low-lying branches. It was hard to tell who it was, but it appeared female.

Pierson squinted. "Well, it looks like it could be Mrs. Mathison. It's her house."

"We've sent for the fire department to get a ladder to get up there. There's a ladder around back, but we can't get to the body because of the chimney and those branches from that side." She looked at Pierson. "And I didn't want to move the ladder in case..."

Pierson raised an eyebrow.

"In case, we needed to look for evidence."

"For evidence? You think we have a crime here, Officer? Nobody kills anybody in this town. The most serious crimes we've got are shoplifting candy bars by teenagers."

"It is a body on a roof, sir."

"You're aware that Mrs. Mathison calls us, or the fire department, at least once a month to get her cat off her roof. And possibly sometimes does it herself in between." He let his eyes roam the rest of the roof. "There! You see that just at the corner of the chimney? There's Reginald now." He turned back to Reasoner. "She probably thought she could handle it herself again this time – to keep somebody else from coming out in the bad weather."

"It is a body on a roof, sir. And it was a bad storm last night. I can't see her going out for her cat in that."

Pierson slowly nodded. "You may be right, Speed. I just hope she hasn't been lying up there not dead, just unconscious, waiting for us to get another ladder."

Reasoner looked stricken. "The body really looks dead. Oh my God, the report just said, 'dead body'. I didn't think to check it..."

"Apparently neither did Bud." He pointed to Addams, who was Bud because Pierson couldn't think of anything else to call him and he was already Bud to everyone else. "Or the joggers." Then gestured to the other neighbors. "Or anyone else. So maybe we better take a look. Just to make sure?"

At that moment the fire truck pulled up, causing a murmur among the crowd, who probably hadn't even been thinking fire.

"Let's get that ladder and see just what we have up there. Bud!" He called to the other officer. "Have them back that truck up to that corner. We're going to meet them on top."

While Addams, only a few years younger than Reasoner but already starting to put on a little weight, was directing the fire truck to a good spot to reach the body, Pierson walked around the back of the house, with Reasoner following. He went straight to the ladder, looked up at the roof, then reset the ladder closer to where they could reach Mrs. Mathison, or whoever. He placed one foot on the bottom rung and tested his weight before climbing to the roof. Reasoner seemed to hesitate, but followed in her boss' steps.

Pierson wiped his hands as he stood leaning into the peak, then strode purposefully, or as purposefully as one can on a pitched roof, to the chimney, resting his hand on the top to balance himself. He reached down with the other and plucked the cowering Reginald up. The cat was so drenched that it didn't even complain, but lowly mewed and lay limp as a rag.

He handed the cat to Reasoner. "Here, find someone down there with a towel and try to dry him off. I'll go look at Mrs....." He stopped after a step and looked back. "Just as a question, did anybody ring the doorbell to see if Mrs. Mathison was in the house?"

"Yes, sir, there was no answer."

He gave her a thumbs up. "OK, then I'll go check on what is probably Mrs. Mathison."

He stepped over the peak just as the fire ladder was arriving from the other side. He brushed some more piles of wet leaves, picked something shiny up, looked at it for a second, and put it in his pocket. He bent down next to the vent and tugged the shoulder of the body over to him so he could see the face.

An EMT poked his head over the edge of the roof.

"Yeah, Jim, it's Grace Mathison. Damn." Pierson put his head down for a moment. "And she's dead." He started to shift the body and sighed. "Can we get her down your ladder there?"

"Chief Pierson." Reasoner was right behind him, with no cat. That was pretty quick, he thought. That's why I call her Speed. "This is a death under suspicious circumstances. We have to call the county coroner."

Pierson sighed and looked at the EMT, Jim McGarry, who had now joined him beside the body. Jim shrugged and whispered, "By the book, is she?"

"Officer Reasoner, you are correct. I hate to leave her up here to the elements, though. Make that call quick, and see if we can get a tarp or something to cover her up."

The call was made, the coroner confirmed he was on his way, and a tarp was found. Pierson spent a few moments next to the body and walking the apparent path from where the ladder had first been to the vent, and finally descended to the ground.

He tried the back door next to the ladder, found it unlocked, and opened it to go inside. Reasoner followed him in.

"What are you doing?" she whispered, feeling like they were breaking in.

"The house is open. If you think there is more to this than meets the eye, then let's see if anything was going on in here."

He looked around the kitchen. "Not much here. A couple of glasses." He picked up one. "Do you think it's suspicious that there's more than one glass, officer?"

She bent down and looked carefully at the floor on the other side of the kitchen table, reached out and ran her finger across a spot.

"It's damp here. But she didn't come back in after going out. Not if she died out there."

"Unless it's from us, just now."

"You didn't walk over here on this side of the room."

Pierson shrugged and slightly shook a sleeve. Water sprayed everywhere, including where he hadn't walked. He continued into the living area, what would have been a family room if she had family living with her, but now was just where Mrs. Mathison had done much of her single living. Running his hand along the surfaces, he walked throughout the room, occasionally picking up an object, then putting it back down.

"Wait!" Reasoner called from the doorway.

He took another step before turning to look at her.

She pointed. "That looked like a wet spot there, but you just stepped into it."

"Speed – Stephanie – I've been walking all over this room. There are plenty of wet spots. All mine." He waved his arms to include the entire room. "I don't see anything missing. At least there are no blank spaces." He rubbed a corner of the mantel. "And I don't see anything disturbed. If you want to go through the rest of the house, go ahead. I doubt if you'll find anything here." As she moved past him, he continued, "But, if you do, let me know."

He walked back through the kitchen and out the back door, stepping foot on the lawn just as Officer Addams came around the corner, leading a man, mustached and middle-aged, which, in Pierson's mind, made him older than Pierson himself.

He held out his hand. "Pete, sorry to bring you out in this, but there's a body on the roof, and we don't get too many of those."

Dr. Peter Ross shook his hand. "Would think the body would rather be down here in a nice warm bed, wouldn't you? But, I take 'em where I get 'em." Ross headed to the ladder and up.

Pierson turned to Addams. "Bud, are the EMTs still here?" At Addams' nod, he said, "Go ask them if they can stick around for a little while, unless there really is a fire or emergency somewhere else. We will still need their ladder and their help to get Mrs. Mathison down after Doc Ross is done. And then," he pulled out his wallet and gave Addams a couple of bills, "go get some coffees for everybody, what, six-seven of us now? At Mac's Café down the street. You know what we want and ask them what they'd like."

He then went up the ladder to join the doctor.

Ross was already bent over the body, but hadn't touched anything yet.

"Anyone move the body? Position looks even more unnatural than I would have thought."

"Yeah, I checked to see if there was any way she was still alive. She wasn't. Then I started to shift it to take it down before we realized we better wait for you. Sorry."

Ross just shook his head. "Probably not much harm done. Don't think it made her any deader than she was already. But don't do it again."

He pulled on gloves and spent a few more moments examining the body itself, then the area around it, up to the spot from which a slip was likely to have occurred, seemingly trying to determine just how the death could have happened.

"Not much more I can do here." He tugged the gloves off. "Don't see anything yet that would indicate foul play. Probably broke something when she slipped, or lost consciousness and died from the elements. But have somebody take some pictures, and I'll take a better look at her when I get her on a table." He waved to another man on the ground. "Jerry would normally take the pictures, but I happen to know he's scared to death of heights. So to speak. Can give his camera to someone else."

Pierson nodded. "I'm sure Officer Reasoner would be glad to help. She'll take every angle she can think of."

They descended to the ground. Addams was already handing out the coffees. Doctor Ross refused his. "Don't drink coffee. Seen too many things between my practice and this side job that I don't need any help staying awake. I'll take a look at her later and let you know if there's anything different."

He walked away as Reasoner came out of the house. Pierson raised his eyebrows in a question at her, and she shook her head in return. She moved closer and inclined her head toward Ross' back. "He's done already?"

Pierson shrugged. "Not much he can really do here once he's taken a look at the body. Can you get a camera from Jerry and go up there to take some pictures? He doesn't like heights. Take shots of the body from some different angles and of the roof between her ladder and her. Anything you can think of."

He walked to the small group of men sitting on the side of the fire truck. "Bud, you've got the statements from the joggers?" Addams gave him a quick nod and held up a notebook. "Good. Then you can send them home. After Speed comes back down, the three of you," he included the EMTs, "can bring the body down and get it over to Doctor Ross. Just don't drop it. We don't want any unexplained bruises or fractures. Any more of them, I should say. I'm going back to the office and find out what else the storm brought us."

# CHAPTER 2

Pierson sent the only other Summerfield officer, George "Pops" Peabody, to supervise the moving of a tree that had fallen across the street next to the elementary school. More to keep the students from gawking at it than it being a real nuisance, but might as well get it done. Peabody had been with the department longer than Pierson, longer than anyone tried to remember, but he kept saying he had nowhere else to go, and he took on most of the busy work that couldn't be avoided. Which was fine with everybody.

A lot of complaint calls related to the storm had come in, but most of them could be handled by a single phone call or a referral to the town's maintenance department, run by Sally Grochuk. Once people had complained to her, they usually wished they hadn't. She took care of the problem, one way or another, as the woman who complained about a delay in getting the snow plowed off her street discovered when the next storm's snowfall was immediately all dumped in front of her driveway.

A quick few hours later, Dr. Ross walked into the chief's office and threw himself down in a chair.

Pierson raised his eyebrows. "You don't look happy. Something besides the weather and an older woman dying from exposure. An unexpected problem?"

"Didn't hit her on the head, did you?"

Pierson paused, then slowly shook his head.

"Didn't think so." Ross took a deep breath and blew it back out.

"Her skull has been shattered, just over the left temple. By a rounded object. Nothing on the roof to cause that, not the corner of the chimney or the vent. Afraid you're going to have to send someone out to take a closer look at the roof and the grounds below it. Couldn't have gotten up to the roof with that wound, and can't explain it with what's up there and the position of the body. Can't rule it an accidental death at this point."

It was Pierson's turn to sigh. "Oh, hell. You mean we might really have a murder here? Mrs. Mathison?"

"Unless you can come up with something at the scene that explains it otherwise."

"Damn. The more I thought about it, but I was hoping..." Ross raised an eyebrow. Pierson raised and dropped a hand. "I'm going to have to apologize to Speed. She was right about not disturbing things. And I'm going to have to get the county crime scene guys out there right away. They're not going to be happy about the mess we made this morning, on top of all the rain."

He spun in his chair to look out the window. "We haven't had a homicide in this town for, what, six years? Who would have thought? Mrs. Mathison wouldn't hurt a fly. Not Mrs. Mathison." He turned back. "You sure there isn't any way it could have been an accident?" At the headshake, he went on. "What happened there, Doc? An older lady and her cat on a roof in a storm. What could have led to that?"

Ross shook his head again. "You'll find out. Not many secrets in this town. But it's going to be hard to figure why. May never know that." He stood up. "Got some things to finish up. Ladder still leaning against the roof? Might take another look myself."

Pierson snorted. "Probably. I never told anybody to take it down."

After Ross left, Pierson sat for a minute, then slowly walked to the door of his office. "Hazy!" He called for Marie Hazlett, the secretary-receptionist-dispatcher-"fill-in-for-whatever-is-needed" for the department. "Get hold of Reasoner, Addams, and Peabody, and tell them to meet in Room A in..." He looked at his watch "...an hour and a half. You too." He closed his door behind him as he stepped out. "Also, call the Lincoln County crime scene unit and get them out to the Mathison house. Doc Ross will be there and can fill them in." He sighed. "There's something I better take care of first."

— — —

Mrs. Grace Mathison didn't have any children, but she did have a nephew in town. Harry Townsend hadn't been in Summerfield long; his aunt had arranged for a job interview for him with the Johnson & Johnson Insurance Company about six months before. It was rumored that she and Mel

Johnson had always had an unfulfilled thing for each other, and that he would likely do anything for her. So Mel interviewed her nephew and, finding nothing immediately objectionable and a willingness to learn the business, hired him.

As the insurance office was only three buildings down (almost everything to do with business in town was on one side of the green or the other), Pierson walked to it. He expected to find Harry in his office with a window overlooking the green, either with a client or doing paperwork. Reports were that he was fairly successful in the business, so he should be busy with something. But he probably didn't know about his aunt yet.

"No, he doesn't have a client right now, Chief Pierson." Sherri Northrup, the receptionist, smiled at him. "Are you looking for some insurance? Maybe life insurance in your line of work? You never know."

"No, Sherri, the city pays for that. I just need to talk with Harry for a moment, if you don't mind. But you might want to make sure we're not disturbed."

"Oh, personal stuff, huh? Or legal, maybe?" Her smile broadened. Sherri was at the center of much of Summerfield's gossip. If she didn't know it, it hadn't happened yet. But apparently, Mrs. Mathison's death was too new even for her. "Come on back." She stood up and led Pierson down the hall to Harry's office.

Mel Johnson was standing in the doorway, apparently just chatting with Townsend because they didn't appear to mind the interruption. Johnson looked fit for his age, but retirement was just around the corner. Townsend was closer to thirty than forty and husky, as if football had been in his background.

Mel put out his hand. "Hello, Jeff. Good to see you. I think. I hope you're not here to arrest my best agent."

Townsend started at that remark as he stood, but quickly put on his best customer smile and also reached out a hand. "Chief Pierson. What does bring you out on such a fine day?"

Pierson inwardly grimaced at the client-pleasing comment. A fine day? Hasn't he looked out the window? And he's certainly not going to continue with that thought after he hears what I'm here to tell him.

"No, no, I'm not arresting anybody. Nobody's in trouble. But," he paused, "I'm afraid I do have some bad news for Mr. Townsend. Mel, if it's okay with Harry, you might as well stay to hear this."

He looked from one to the other and took a deep breath. "Mr. Townsend, there isn't any good way to say this, but your aunt's body was found this morning. She died sometime last night."

Townsend abruptly sat back down. Johnson leaned back hard against the wall and pulled out a handkerchief. The breath appeared to be knocked out of him.

Townsend was the first to respond. "Aunt Grace?" At Pierson's nod, "You say her body? What do you mean? Did she die in her sleep?" He put his hand to his mouth. "Was it a heart attack?"

Pierson shook his head.

"A stroke? A fall?"

"Her body was found on the roof."

That drew a startled "What?" from both Townsend and Johnson.

"At first we thought she had gone up to get her cat during the storm, had slipped and knocked herself unconscious, then died from exposure. A couple of joggers saw her on the roof early this morning. But then Dr. Ross examined her and found that she had been struck on the head by some object that doesn't fit anything up there. So it looks like somebody hit her somewhere else and put the body on the roof."

"Somebody...put the body...on the roof? What the...?" Townsend was having trouble getting the words out.

"We don't know what or why yet. But we've started a complete investigation. We will try to figure this out."

"Harry," Johnson finally appeared to have recovered his speech and stepped towards Townsend. "We'll find out what's going on." He turned to Pierson. "Is there anything else you can tell us, Jeff? As you can see, Harry's in shock right now." He wiped his brow with the handkerchief. "We both are. Oh my, I, I don't know what to say. But please keep us up on everything you find out." He stood up straighter. "Whatever you need from us, let us know."

Pierson shook his head. "No, there's nothing else at the moment, we will be back in touch. Mr. Townsend, I want you to know that we are truly sorry for your loss. I knew your aunt, and we all liked her."

"Yes, everybody liked her." Townsend slowly nodded. "Who would hit her? About anything?"

"I agree. No one would want to hurt her."

"Where is she now?"

"She's at the coroner's office – in the back room of Dr. Ross' practice. But she may be moved to the facilities in Oldstown, if Dr. Ross feels it's warranted."

There was a silent moment as the three of them had run out of things to say and each spent time in their own thoughts.

"Harry, give me a minute as I walk Chief Pierson out." Johnson's hand shook slightly as he took Pierson's arm and led him to the outer reception area. "Jeff, please keep me informed on what's happening. Grace was ... very special to me. And, just so you know, though I'm positive he had absolutely nothing to do with it, Harry was out of town with a client last night. I am pretty sure of that. If you need to know the details, we can probably get them verified, but I know he wasn't anywhere around here."

"Thanks, Mel. I am sorry for your loss too. At this time, we just don't know anything about what happened. I'll let you know."

# CHAPTER 3

The entire police department for Summerfield fit around the table in Conference Room A. Conference Room B was actually used for storage more than anything else, but calling it *Room A* instead of "*the conference room*" sounded more professional and gave the impression that there were other conference room options available for important meetings.

Nobody needed to be reminded of the meeting and, for one of the few times that Pierson could recall, no one was late. He walked to what was usually considered the head of the table and faced his team.

"You may, or may not know by now that Mrs. Mathison's death does not appear to be accidental. At least according to Pete Ross, and we have no reason to question his findings. She was apparently struck on the head by a round object that doesn't fit anything found on the roof, and her body, we are assuming at this point, was placed there possibly, probably after death. Nothing is certain yet, except that she is dead and it is suspicious, as Officer Reasoner originally asserted. Steph, I do owe you an apology. I should have dealt with this more seriously from the beginning." He glanced at Reasoner, but her face showed nothing. Apparently, she was ready to go on to the next step.

He turned to the full-wall chalkboard behind him, erased a message about last summer's department picnic, hesitated a moment but left one about the upcoming downtown Halloween parade, and picked up a dusty piece of chalk. He wrote GRACE MATHISON at the top, then a left-hand column, WHAT IS KNOWN, with "on the roof", "round object – left temple", and "thunderstorm", underneath.

"I'll add to this column as we gain information, and as I think about what's important. But right now we don't have much.

"Speed, I want you to interview Harry Townsend and confirm where he was last night." Pierson wrote another column with her name, then added more columns as he continued to talk. "Pops, you talk to the neighbors, see if they saw or heard anything, besides the storm last night. Also if they have seen or heard anything in the past that could give us any possible reason for Mrs. Mathison's death. Bud, you look through the house, and around the grounds, particularly below where the body was."

Addams spoke up. "What am I looking for, chief? You and Steph went through the house this morning."

"We weren't looking for a murder weapon, or at least a cause of death. I've talked to county forensics and made sure they know what we know. Maybe they have seen something or found something that makes sense, or need to go back again. I don't know what specifically we're looking for except that it is round, but I want you to also be looking for a reason – anything that seems to be out of place or could have led to a motive. Just a general impression at first.

"We have a major investigation now. We've all been trained for it. We just haven't been practicing it. We will figure this out. Hazy, you will coordinate from the office, and organize information by Crime Scene, Suspects, and Motives. We'll figure out more as we get more. Any specific questions at this point?"

Reasoner raised her hand.

"Speed, you don't have to raise your hand. You can just speak out."

"Chief, you mentioned suspects. Do we have any at this time? Anything come up from talking to Mel Johnson or Harry Townsend? You would think that, if anybody knew anything, it might be one of them."

Pierson shook his head. "No, not from our brief conversation last night – I was more informing than interrogating at that time. But that's what we hope to develop from some of the interviewing you and Pops will be doing. I will talk to Mel Johnson. He was probably closer to Mrs. Mathison than anyone else. He and Harry. You're right, if anybody knows any possible motives, it would likely be one of them."

He looked around the room. "Folks, at the beginning we're going to be feeling our way through this. I get that, but this is a small town, and everybody knows everybody. We need to act professional and show them that we do know what we are doing. The townspeople will look to us for trust and guidance. We'll meet again tomorrow morning at nine." He drew a deep breath. "Okay, go to it."

Everybody filed out except for Hazlett.

"Jeff." When no one was around, she felt she could call him by his first name. Actually, she sometimes did it at other times too. Though only a few years older, she had been one of his babysitters when he was little. "Do you want me to rewrite what you have on the board? Your handwriting is still barely legible. In fact, it's gotten worse as you've gotten older."

He looked over his shoulder. "I can read it. Most of it anyway. But you're probably right. No one else can. Go ahead."

He left her to the job of cleaning up after him and headed to his office to come up with a list of questions for Mel Johnson. A list that wasn't going to offend but still needed to get at why someone would want to hurt Grace Mathison and then put her body on the roof. In the pouring rain.

# CHAPTER 4

George Peabody, with a gray moustache, graying hair and the beginning of a paunch all giving away his age, didn't make any list. He was just going to talk, but mostly listen. That was what he was good at doing, asking a question then letting the other person ramble, and everybody on the street knew him well enough to at least say something.

He made a rough visual circle in his head, starting to the left of the Mathison home, going up four houses (that was probably enough, maybe even just three), crossing the street, coming back past the house across from hers to the next intersection and finishing with the two houses between hers and the corner.

No one objected to talking with him – everyone felt comfortable with Pops – and he got halfway through the interviews with the hospitable offers of two cookies, a glass of homemade cider, and a piece of peach pie, but no recognizably helpful information. Nobody had seen anything last night with the storm going on, nobody had heard anything, and nobody could think of any reason why anyone would want to hurt poor old Mrs. Mathison.

Though Mrs. Mathison didn't actually appear to be poor – financially or health-wise. Nobody thought she was wealthy, but she seemed to have enough money to be all right. Ralph Mathison, her husband, had been hit by a car two weeks after his retirement from a management position at the Hepco Paper Company, but he had left a nice pension, and she had her own retirement from teaching second grade for thirty-five years. Her health appeared to be good. She was known as a tough old bird who went on many bird-watching hikes as well as bicycling around town. And she wasn't really that old – maybe in her early sixties, fit and wiry for her age.

But no enemies. No reason for anybody to wish her any ill-will.

Peabody raised his hand toward the bell on Hazel Bucholtz's door, directly across the street from the Mathison home. Hazel was in her early eighties, at least, but had briefly been the principal with Grace Mathison at Kramer Elementary School.

The door opened before he even found out if there was a working doorbell or not.

"Yes, Officer Peabody? May I help you?"

She had a cane and didn't look as if she was afraid to use it. Peabody automatically took his hat off without even being aware of doing it. Mrs. Bucholtz had that effect on people.

"I am sorry to disturb you this afternoon. I am here today in my role as a police officer, investigating last night. Ma'am, are you aware of what has happened across the street?"

"I am aware of everything, young man. At least as far as you are concerned. And who wouldn't have noticed the commotion across the street this morning? Noise and vehicles and people gathering and gawking. Excepting for the fact that Grace is dead, there hasn't been this much excitement on this street since the Winkler's sad attempt at swinging several years ago."

Peabody momentarily wondered now about Ginger Winkler offering him that pie.

"Ma'am, we are asking the neighbors if they happened to have seen or heard anything last night. I know it was very noisy and dark with the storm, but there may have been something that caught your attention."

"You better come in, officer. It is not polite to discuss serious business on the front stoop."

She led him into her front room, which was bright and airy with the afternoon sun coming in the undraped window. Her rocking chair, instead of facing the television, was squarely in front of the window looking across the street.

Peabody walked over to the window and found himself looking at the front of Mrs. Mathison's house, full frontal view. He turned around and discovered Mrs. Bucholtz holding out a glass of lemonade. He had no idea when she had had time to leave the room to get it, nonetheless pour it.

"Homemade?" he asked as he took it.

"Heavens no. My lemon-squeezing days are well behind me. It is from a carton, Wiley's Freshest, as I don't even want to bother with mixing frozen anymore. I do hope that is adequate for you."

"Oh, yes." He took a sip. "That's fine. And thank you. I appreciate it."

"So, officer, please take a seat." She pointed to the bright pink couch, and she turned the rocking chair around to face him before he could offer to help her with it. "You probably want to know if I was watching Grace's house last night.

"As you undoubtedly surmised from the position of my chair, I spend much of my day observing the neighborhood. Much more interesting than the afternoon game shows and those dreadful evening soap operas. For drama, they are incredibly boring, with their extraordinarily petty disagreements and obviously fictional crises. Real people would handle those situations so much better. Absolutely no class." She shook her head.

Pointing out the window, she continued. "I do know Mr. Huffman, the postman, spends much more time at Mrs. Winkler's house than any other. Maybe it's the pie. And the Jeffries' dog, Reuben, is the one digging up the Wolscheimer's woeful tomato plants." She paused. "But that's not why you are here. What did I see last night?" She rocked her chair closer to him. "There was a dreadful storm, you know. Visibility was very poor, but there were flashes of lightning. And in the flashes, I did see a car sitting in her driveway."

Peabody began to ask about the car, but never got the question out.

"It appeared to be a gray four-door sedan. I'm afraid I can't tell anymore what kind of automobile. They keep changing the styles. I never did see anyone get into or out of the car, just that the car was there."

"Any chance of a license plate?" Peabody was making notes in a small Summerfield Police Department notepad.

"Officer, I am not that eagle-eyed in the pouring rain. All I could tell was that it was five characters and there was a large round sticker on the back window. If I had known that she was about to get murdered, I would have picked up my high-powered binoculars for a closer look." She pointed to the stand next to the window, "but I wasn't that prescient." His face must have given away his confusion over the word. "Able to see the future."

"Well, thank you, ma'am. This is still pretty observant. Tell me, have you seen that car before?"

"Not that I know of. There are other gray sedans that have been by, but that is not a vehicle that I have seen in Grace's driveway before."

"What time was this?"

"Ten thirty-three. I had just finished watching an episode of *Washington Slept Here* on my video player and was about to retire for the night."

Thank you again, Mrs. Bucholtz." Peabody was about to tuck his notepad back in his vest pocket. "Is there anything else that you can think of?"

"Not unless you are interested in the outrageous prices at the Peterson's garage sale, or that the Hall boy, Tommy, was smoking in the back yard?" She watched him finish putting the pad away. "No? Then I believe our conversation is completed for the present."

Peabody finished the lemonade. Not bad for store-bought. He'd have to try that brand, "Wiley's" did she say, the next time he went grocery shopping.

He completed the rest of the street. He asked follow-up questions regarding the car, but besides a brownie at the Peterson's, there was nothing worthwhile. Two of the houses had nobody home, but he suspected Mrs. Bucholtz had provided the only meaningful information – the gray sedan.

# CHAPTER 5

Martin Addams stepped through the still unlocked back door of the Mathison home. They hadn't put out the yellow police DO NOT DISTURB tape yet, but he had it in his trunk ready to go. He had noticed George Peabody's car parked on the street next door and, in a way, envied him talking to people that were still alive. There was already a scent of death in the air of this house. At least it smelled that way to him.

He put on a pair of gloves and pulled out the small notebook that they all carried, labeled Summerfield Police Department, Official Log, with Courtesy of Hepco Paper Company in small print at the bottom (the irony of Mrs. Mathison's husband possibly designing these notebooks briefly crossed his mind), and noted the two glasses on the sink. He leaned over to sniff at them, but they had apparently been washed. The floor was now dry (Steph had mentioned the puddles of water, but they weren't there any longer). No chairs pulled out, no indications of anything disturbed. It felt funny to open someone else's cupboards; it was as if he was trespassing into her life, as if Grace Mathison had a right to her own secrets and he had no business knowing them. But a quick look turned up nothing unexpected. He didn't want to disturb anything as the crime scene unit was going to be doing its own deeper inspection later.

Crossing into the small living room, he stopped and let his eyes slowly flow across the room, getting a general sense of Mrs. Mathison's presence and noting if there were any jarring notes, anything that didn't seem to belong.

She had collected a lot of miscellaneous knick-knacks. And maybe collected was the wrong word. Apparently, she just hadn't gotten rid of anything that she had acquired through the years – trip souvenirs, gifts from students, presents from relatives who didn't know what really to get her, so get her something cute. Ceramic animals, cups and mugs, foreign figurines, trophies.

Addams paused at the corner display case. Trophies? Yes, there was a My Favorite Teacher one, but also a golf one and one for basketball. Maybe the golf one was hers or her husband's, but basketball? He leaned in close and saw that it was for a church league, from two years ago. He hadn't personally known Mrs. Mathison, just to greet in the grocery store, but he couldn't picture her playing in a basketball league. He didn't recall any older adult leagues. And he couldn't imagine her coaching, or officiating, or having anything to do with basketball. He supposed it was possible, but it seemed odd to be that recent.

He stepped back and looked around the room again. Now that he was looking for more details, on the mantelpiece was a plaque for salesman of the year from a local car dealer. Next to it, another trophy with a diver perched on top. Three small clocks in different sites. A wooden fish from a fishing tournament. This was more than miscellaneous. Not hoarding, but not pieces that should have come naturally to her – not gifts, not personal keepsakes. Not what you would expect to be personal to her anyway.

As details were becoming clearer, he saw that several shelves were overcrowded, but a few were not. Objects were spaced evenly, but on two shelves there was obviously much less of them. It certainly was possible that something had been taken, but what? And why?

He walked back through the kitchen and out the door. The county crime scene unit was now here again, getting ready to head up to the roof, while one was investigating the ground below the ladder and another below where her body had been on the roof. Two were studying the base of the walls, looking for anything out of the expected. Addams recognized one, a cousin of his.

"Phil! Phil, can you come over here a minute?"

Phil Culbertson looked up, saw who it was, and walked gingerly over, trying not to disturb what was left from what was now a crime scene.

"Yeah, Bud. What can I do for you?"

"I just came from inside. Don't worry," putting up his gloved hands. "I didn't touch anything. Well, except for some cabinet knobs in the kitchen. I just wanted a quick look inside them."

Phil nodded. "We can probably live with that. So long as we know."

"Do you have somebody with a camera?"

"We have several somebodies with cameras. That's what we do." Phil smiled to take the sting out of the comment.

"I guess what I mean is, is somebody going to take pictures inside the house? I'd like to have pictures taken of all the knick-knack cabinets and shelves and bookcases."

"We'll do that. Are you looking for anything in particular? Want close-ups of something?"

"Both distance and close-ups of each shelf. I don't know what I'm looking for. Yet. There seems to be something odd about them. Too many things that don't seem to belong. At least belong to her. But I don't know what that means." Addams shrugged. "If anything."

He turned back to the door. "I'm going to look through more of the house. But I'm not going to touch anything. At least I'm planning on not touching anything, but, if I do, I'll let you know. OK?"

"Yeah, do what you need to do. We really don't expect to find much to help us, with all the people that were here this morning, and no one being careful then. Unless there's a blood splatter somewhere and a weapon just lying around."

"I know Steph was trying to be careful. Maybe she was able to save something. Thanks, Phil."

Addams retraced his steps through the kitchen and living room to the hallway facing the front door. He started to reach out to the door, then decided he better leave it to Phil's team to check for evidence of a possible break-in. Behind him down the hall was another door, which he did open and turned out to be for the basement. He thought he could look at it later. To its left was the hall closet. Deciding he could open that door too, he found fall, winter, spring, and summer coats, apparently rotated by the season. Hats, gloves, a small toolkit, and two flashlights on the shelf. One box behind them.

Okay, I'm going to have to touch something, he thought to himself. He pulled the box down and found it contained toy soldiers. Surprised, he set it on the floor. Now he realized he had also seen a couple of soldier figures on one of the shelves in the living room. When you see one or two, you figure it represents a trip or something of particular historical significance, but a boxful? Not intended to play with -- they didn't look old enough to be childhood toys for Mr. or Mrs. Mathison or even her nephew, and he hadn't heard about any children. Maybe there were younger relatives that no one was aware of yet.

Leaving the box where it was to ensure the photographers getting it, he moved to the hall opposite. Master bedroom to the right. Stepping in, it was clear that these mementos were more personal...family pictures, reading books, a couple of jewelry boxes on a dresser. He gently lifted the lid of both boxes and discovered them full of necklaces and earrings, but there was no way Addams could tell if anything was of value or if any jewelry was missing. But then he didn't think there was any way you could have crammed anything else in. He glanced around the corner at the bathroom. It looked typical and undisturbed. The medicine cabinet held extra toothbrushes and toothpaste, cough medicine, and heartburn pills. No prescriptions. They were going to have to check her health history to determine if any drugs should have been there, but were not.

In the hallway, the door opposite led to what appeared to be Mrs. Mathison's study/workroom. The window on the far wall now glowed with sunlight, indicating the storm had completely passed. There was a desk against the left wall topped with bills and personal papers. A table stood in the middle of the room with two chairs set up to it. A sewing machine sat on it, and sewing paraphernalia was scattered around the machine. Mrs. Mathison's apparent hobby. Opening the closet to the right revealed more sewing materials and out-of-season clothes.

At the end of the hallway, a bathroom was to the right, again nothing particularly out of place, and what appeared to be the smallest room opposite. It included a small dresser and a single guest bed, seemingly not used in quite some time, and a tall bookshelf against the back wall. It had a few books, but also the rest of the collection of miscellaneous doodads and whatnots. No real order or sense of belonging to any of them. The closet to the left was mostly empty, but held a few older men's jackets and ties. Probably some of Ralph's things that Grace had never been able to bring herself to get rid of.

Addams had seen enough to rule out a random break-in and any sort of a search for valuables. If there had been anything of real value, it was going to take a record of it in her paperwork or her nephew recognizing it was gone, and someone that had known exactly where and what it was.

Passing the master bedroom again, he glanced back in and, this time, noticed a framed picture on the dresser of Grace Mathison and her nephew, Harry Townsend. In the picture, they were standing to one side of the mantle in the living room with a portrait of Ralph behind them, and the corner knick-knack shelf on the other side of them. To Addams, it looked much more symmetrical, the shelves more evenly distributed than now. He picked up the picture carefully by one corner and took it back with him to the living room.

Holding it up next to the cabinet, now he could see that there were some obvious pieces missing. What appeared to be a bowling trophy, a small statue of two objects (was that Laurel and Hardy?), a wooden bowl, and a toy locomotive. Maybe some other tiny items, but there were definitely differences. They certainly didn't appear to be worth much, definitely not someone's life, but it was something to start with. Maybe they had been given away at some point, but maybe not.

# CHAPTER 6

Stephanie Reasoner retraced Pierson's steps toward the Johnson & Johnson Insurance office. The main north-south street through town (for some reason known as North Main and South Main) split to go around the town green, the pastoral heart of Summerfield. A bandstand, used for summer Monday Night Musical Memory concerts and Fourth of July parade announcements, stood in the center. It wasn't big enough to hold more than ten performers, particularly if they used instruments, but it was still the centerpiece of the shows, giving the director a place to stand and the town council a place to sit. An open space remained in front of it, large enough for concert seating and volleyball games during family picnics. Trees stood behind it and throughout the green, sharing space with a few picnic tables and benches.

Along the west side stood the police station and the rest of the town hall, a dentist office, a hardware store, the insurance office, Summerfield National Bank, and a few other shops and small offices. The east side held the Summerfield Church of Light and Hope, Mac's Café, the Summerfield Press, and again the necessary sundry shops and offices, including Mayor Plummer's law office, which was in use when he wasn't busy mayoring.

In nice weather, Reasoner ate her lunch at one of the scattered picnic tables and enjoyed watching the townspeople go about their business. Today had not been one of those days.

She entered the waiting area of the insurance office and stepped up to Sherri Northrup sitting at the front desk. There was only the one Johnson in Johnson & Johnson, but the story was that somewhere along the line Mel had thought that adding another one made it sound more professional and prosperous.

"Hi, Steph." They had been classmates in high school. "Are you here to see Harry? That is such a shame. I didn't really know Mrs. Mathison, but she seemed like a nice person. His aunt, you know."

"Sherri." Reasoner nodded. "Is he here? I know the chief was here earlier, but there are just a few questions I need to ask him. And it might be more comfortable here than at the station or his home."

"Harry's in his office. I don't think he's done much of anything, and Mel told him to leave, but he said he didn't know where he'd go. Nothing at home, and it's not like he's a drinking man. At least not at this time of day. I don't know about evenings or when he's with a client. He doesn't tell me about them. I think Mel's going over to Mac's to meet with your boss a little later. Everybody's in demand today."

Reasoner interrupted. "Okay if I go back to his office? You can let him know I'm coming."

"Sure thing. I like doing it official-like, like this is a big important office or something."

Sherri gave the call and pointed down the hall in the direction of his office, and Reasoner walked towards his door.

Townsend was sitting at his desk, but not paying any attention to the papers on top of it. He was working a squeeze ball in one hand, but didn't seem to really be aware of that either.

"Mr. Townsend, I'm Officer Reasoner. If you're up to it, I'd like to ask you a few questions regarding your aunt."

"Yeah." He passed the ball to the other hand. "I might as well. I'm not doing anything much worthwhile here. Oh, just so you know we have met before. Mel Johnson introduced us at lunch one time. And I would find it hard to forget you. A lovely woman in uniform is memorable. Please sit down and make yourself comfortable."

Reasoner paused for a second, then sat. The "lovely woman in uniform" wasn't a comment she had been expecting. Inwardly she shrugged. Maybe this was how he handled uncomfortable situations – retreating into his salesman persona, including some hopefully harmless flirting.

"I do wish to express my condolences on your loss. I didn't know Mrs. Mathison well, but she appeared to be a very nice woman, and everyone else speaks highly of her."

"Thank you. She was. She took good care of me when I came to town, and we spent time together several evenings a week." He resumed squeezing the ball.

She pulled out her department notebook. "May I ask just how you were related?"

"My father was her brother. Her maiden name was Grace Townsend. My parents have been gone for a few years, so she has been the closest thing to a mother for me recently."

"Are there any other relatives?"

"I have a sister in Colorado. She's married, name is now Ann Bennett if you need it, and she has two children. I called and told her this morning after Chief Pierson was here. She will probably be coming to town in a few days when she has arranged for time off. I believe there was family on Uncle Ralph's side, but I only met them at his funeral and have never had any other contact with them. They're from somewhere south, but I couldn't tell you where."

He shifted in his seat. "Can you tell me any more about what happened? Chief Pierson just said she was found on her roof, that she had been hit on the head with something and her body had been placed there?" He seemed to have trouble referring to "her body".

"That is all that we are aware of at this time, sir. Outside of the roof part, the rest is primarily conjecture, nothing proven yet. The county crime scene unit is out there now, and we have officers canvassing the neighborhood to see if anybody saw anything last night. "

"In the rain? Good luck with that." He sat forward. "The chief said they thought at first that she had gone out on the roof to get her cat? Why would anybody think that? She wasn't senile, officer."

"Mrs. Mathison had a history of needing to get her cat off the roof. She had called both the police and the fire department several times, and it was thought that she might not have wanted to disturb them again." Reasoner decided she needed to retake control of the conversation. "There was a ladder against the roof in back. Do you know if she had a ladder that would have reached?"

"Yes, she did." Townsend rubbed his forehead. "I have had to use it on occasion. There were times I was called for the cat too. But I have never known her to go out on her own. She wasn't comfortable with heights."

"I didn't know that. At first, as I said, we thought she may have been trying to do this on her own, but now we know that was not the case."

"Now I'm wondering if she tried to call me about the cat. I wasn't home last night." He took a deep breath. "If I had been, maybe she would still be alive."

"Sir, we don't know the circumstances from last night yet. Don't beat yourself up."

"It's Harry, Officer Reasoner. In this community, I don't think we need to be as formal. The sirs make me feel guilty about everything. Do you have a first name, or is it Officer?" He smiled.

"My name is...Stephanie, sir, uh, Harry, um, Mr. Townsend. But I don't believe this is the appropriate time. I would prefer Officer Reasoner at this point. I'm sorry. This is our first suspicious death, and I am trying to be professional. And I probably shouldn't have used the term 'suspicious death'".

"That's okay, but it does sound grim."

Reasoner felt like she had lost control of the interview once again. "To get back to the point of my visit, unless something different turns up today, it doesn't look like there was any forced entry. There were two glasses recently washed on the kitchen counter. Do you know if she was expecting any company last night? Any friends, any appointments?"

He shook his head. "She, of course, had friends, but I don't know if any would have been over last night. She belonged to a book club. Well, they called it a book club, but they usually went to dinner or over to each other's house and talked about anything and everything. Maybe even books, but mostly about what was going on in Summerfield that you weren't supposed to know was going on. But I think they met on Tuesdays. Not last night." He shifted again in his seat. "I am surprised about the two glasses. I know, because I have asked her about it, that she tended to use just one glass throughout the day. She got one out for juice in the morning and didn't want to dirty another one. Ralph used to get a new one out each time he wanted a sip of water, and that used to bug the hell out of her. And she didn't wash it till the next day when she set it with the breakfast dishes."

"So it would have been unusual for her to have washed glasses sitting on the counter at night?"

"If they were the only thing and when getting ready for bed, yes."

"And you mentioned that you were out of town last night. Can you elaborate on that?" Reasoner tried to make that sound nonchalant, but wasn't sure if she was successful.

Townsend rubbed his chin this time, looked out the window, took a deep breath and turned back to Reasoner.

"As a gentleman, I'd rather not." He left it hanging, but when she didn't respond, he sighed and continued. "I was with a client in New Lincoln, a female client. And I stayed the night. Mel knows about it." He pulled a pad toward him and wrote on it. "Here's her name and number. She is unmarried, so it's not that there's a husband involved, it's just that..."

"She's not the only one?" Reasoner finished for him. "We will try to be discreet."

"Thank you. The relationship is not serious, and it's not exclusive." There was a hopeful note in there that Reasoner chose to ignore.

"But one of the others may view your relationship with them differently. I'm not going to say I understand, but I am going to say it's not my business. If it doesn't have anything to do with your aunt's death."

She changed the direction of her questions. "Do you know who benefits from Mrs. Mathison's death?"

"Well, nobody benefits. If you mean who inherits, I suppose my sister and I, unless she chose to add any of Ralph's family or Ann's kids in her will. I doubt his family, but I really don't know. I honestly don't know what value there is to it. I never thought about it. If you're thinking I benefit from her death, I can tell you, I'd much rather have her alive. I benefited more from our relationship."

Reasoner raised her eyebrows in an implied question.

"When I first came to town, I didn't know anybody. She told me she thought she could get me a job. And she did, with Mel Johnson. And it's been great. It has really worked out for me." He shrugged his shoulders. "It's also been good to have family. I needed some...stability in my life. My previous circumstances were not the best. I got a brand new start here, and she is, was a big part of it."

"What about her life insurance?"

Townsend half-smiled. "Mel handled that before I came to town. I made sure to stay out of any of those issues with her. I never asked him or her."

Reasoner let that go for the moment.

"Speaking of Mr. Johnson, and this is going to seem very personal, but I have to ask it anyway, what can you tell me about their relationship? It is no secret that there was something there."

Townsend scratched his nose and swiveled slightly in his chair. "I know they cared for each other deeply, but I don't know if it was ever going further than their getting together a couple of times a week, maybe going on a weekend trip. I think Mel may have wanted more, but I also think Aunt Grace was happy with the way things were. If Mel wanted to go to a movie or dinner or some special event, it was going to be with Aunt Grace. If she wanted to do something, I, or even a member of the book club, was still an option for her. They both seemed to be happy, and I'm not aware of any troubles between them. I certainly can't see Mel either hitting her or taking her up on a roof, for heaven's sake."

"You're not aware of any other conflicts? Any disagreements with anybody else?"

"No," he emphatically shook his head. "As I said, she was liked by everybody. I can't imagine anyone doing this. Her friends certainly wouldn't have been physically able to take her on the roof, and somebody breaking into the house to rob it wouldn't have bothered. Would they?"

When Reasoner didn't answer, he continued. "If you want my honest opinion, I think it had to have been an accident, but I couldn't tell you why or how she ended up on that roof. It just doesn't make any sense."

# CHAPTER 7

Jeff Pierson opened the door to Mac's Café and stepped slowly in, as if reluctant to bring any of the tragedy in with him. But he straightened his shoulders and nodded to "Mac" MacIntyre, the proprietor and former football star at Bradford State University, and the reason for the implied "Big" in "Mac's", who simply pointed to Pierson's usual booth. Mel Johnson, in response to an earlier phone call, was already there and Pierson slid in across from him.

"Mel."

"Jeff."

Mac brought a platter over and set it in front of Johnson. It looked like the Bigger Mac Cheeseburger Plate with applesauce and onion rings. He turned to Pierson. "What'll you have, Jeff? The same?"

"No, it's getting close to dinner time, and I'm going to be missing it at home. I'd rather have a full dinner-type meal. Judy's already pissed, and she's not likely to be saving me any from our supper. What's your meatloaf special today, Mac?"

"The Spicy Mexican Meatloaf with guacamole between the outer and inner layers. With rice and refried beans."

Pierson rolled his eyes. "No, that's a bit much for me today. I'll have the Hawaiian Meatloaf with the pineapples. But the rice and beans sound good. And a lemonade to drink."

Johnson hadn't started eating his burger and seemed to be more playing with the food than ingesting it. He took out a handkerchief and blew his nose.

"Rough day, Mel. I really hated to break the news to you that way, but I didn't want to wait any longer before telling the two of you, and I needed to see how Harry was going to react. How are you doing? Really?"

Johnson took a deep breath, then slowly let it out. "When my wife, Janine, died from cancer, about eight years ago, I figured that was going to be the worst thing that would ever happen to me." He picked up an onion ring then put it back down. "It was. I cared for Grace, I suppose you could say I loved her, but I'm surprised I'm not having a stronger reaction. I guess it has to do with our ages, and that we hadn't made any sort of real commitment...and the length of time I was with Janine. I just always thought I'd go first. I'm sort of numb – I'm in shock, I think, more because of how she died than the actual loss. Maybe I'll grieve more later."

He looked back up at Pierson. "I know you have a job to do, Jeff. And I want you to catch the son-of-a-bitch that did this. So ask what you must, and I will answer what I can."

At that moment, Marge, Mac's wife and the primary reason for the success of the café, brought Pierson's dinner. The meatloaf dinner always seemed to be ready as soon as you ordered it.

Pierson picked up his fork. "Eat something, Mel, I'll try to make this as painless as possible. I know you didn't have anything to do with this. Trust me, I'm not going to question your whereabouts."

"I was at home watching TV until I went to bed around 10:30. I don't know when she was supposed to have died, but that's what I was doing. No one else to alibi me." Pierson started to hold up a hand, but Johnson waved him off. "I know, I know, but I wanted to tell you. We don't, didn't, see each other every evening, just when there was something specific to do, or we just wanted company." He folded his handkerchief over and ran it across his mouth. "I wish there had been something last night. But there wasn't."

"You mentioned that you knew Harry had been somewhere else last night."

"Yeah, I did." He laughed, but there was no humor in it. "Harry has a way with people, particularly the ladies. Particularly lonely ladies. It makes him a good salesman. I don't always approve, but then I'm aware I'm an old fogey, and my standards are not the same as the younger generations. He was with a client in New Lincoln, making sure that 'her needs are being met' is how he'd put it. She apparently has frequent 'needs', as she often calls the office to make an appointment to meet with him. And Sherri has him scheduled to meet with her last night. I know you will want to check with her. Sherri has her name and number."

Pierson nodded. "Okay. Do you know anything about Harry's relationship with Grace?"

"As near as I can tell, it was very strong. More like mother-son. I know that doesn't always mean good, but I believe they were very close. I'm not aware of any conflict between them. Certainly not anything that would have led to this. I know he cared for her very much. She was the reason he's in Summerfield. And, as you probably know, she got him this job."

"Can you tell me about that?"

"She told me she had a nephew who was moving into town and needed a job. As you likely know, there really is no 'and Johnson'. I was wanting to wind down and not put as much into the work, so it made sense for me to add somebody younger. And actually, he does fine. Outside of those, ahem, personal relationships with some clients, his work has been very good. I'm glad to have hired him, and I have often told Grace that."

"Did you ever check on his background? Any references?"

"He brought a resume. Was an assistant manager in a department store. And references. But I never really checked on him. He was Grace's nephew and wanted to move into Summerfield, and that was enough for me. As I said, I have had no problem with him and no reason to worry about him."

"Grace have any other close friends? Acquaintances?"

Johnson took a bite of his burger. Talking seemed to help him get back a sense of normalcy.

"She had her book club, but that wasn't last night. And there were friends from church and from when she was teaching. If someone was over last night, I wouldn't necessarily have known. I don't think she had much contact with neighbors, except for Miss Bucholtz across the street. But Miss Bucholtz certainly wouldn't have gone out in last night's weather."

"No, last night was a good night for people not to be out," Pierson agreed. "One last question -- about insurance benefits. I assume she had some life insurance. And I'm guessing with you."

"Yes, she did. Not a lot. She didn't have anyone dependent on her. But what she did have will go to Harry and his sister, Ann, out in Colorado. It's certainly not enough to kill for, believe me. Maybe enough to cover funeral expenses." He pulled out an envelope from an inner pocket of his jacket and slid it across the table to Pierson. "This is a copy of her policy. I figured you'd be asking about it."

"And her will?"

"Matt Laurenfeld is her attorney. She never talked with me about it. I would expect the bulk of it to go to Harry and Ann again. I have no idea of the size of the inheritance, but I don't think it would be much."

Pierson nodded. Apparently, Townsend would have needed more of a motive than money. "Thanks, Mel. I do appreciate your time. And, again, I am personally so sorry for what happened to Grace. Believe me. I wish she were still alive for you."

Pierson finished the rest of his beans and noticed that Johnson had now cleaned his plate, so something had been accomplished by this meeting anyway, even if it hadn't led to any clues as to Mrs. Mathison's death. This day was long, but it was becoming very apparent that it wasn't done yet.

# CHAPTER 8

Pierson, tired and depressed, drove the few blocks to his home following the meeting with Mel Johnson. Not the way he wanted a day to go. He pulled into the driveway, turned off the engine, and sat for a minute, needing to gather himself before heading inside.

Judy met him at the door, anxious to hear what was happening, but knowing better than to push him when he wasn't ready.

"Hi, honey. Are you okay?" She bit her lower lip, a sign that Pierson recognized as the beginning of an anxiety that he needed to soften. "Can you tell me anything?"

That morning, he shared with her briefly about Mrs. Mathison's death and had just told her he didn't know when he would be home. In the family room to his left, he could hear the television.

"JoAnn in there?" When Judy nodded, he pointed to the living room to the right, used only for guests. "Let's go in this room."

They sat on the couch, and he leaned back, expelling a long breath that felt as if he had been holding it all day.

"Not much that I can say. Pops and Speed and Bud have all been out interviewing what is probably half the town and checking out the house. The crime scene people have been all through the house and grounds. I'll hear in the morning if they found out anything vital. I'm guessing not, or they would have called me." He cocked an eye. "Or did somebody call here?"

Judy shook her head. "I've gotten calls from some people, but just wanting to know if I'd heard about the body on the roof, or, if I had, did I know anything more. Just trying to see if I had any information that they didn't have."

"Yeah," he said, but before he could continue, the phone rang.

"I'll get it," Judy rose and moved to the phone on the side table. "Hello? ... Yes, Carol. ... He just got home. ... No, there's nothing new. ... Maybe we'll know more tomorrow. ... Yes, I'll let you know. ... Thank you, good-bye." She hung up the receiver. "Carol Ledbetter." Pierson looked in the direction of the Ledbetter's house across the street. "She saw your car pull in."

"Didn't take long."

"I think everybody's anxious to know. It's a small town. Everyone's heard something about it by now."

"And about it being suspicious, probably a murder?" Jeff grimaced as he said the word.

Judy bit her lip again and nodded. "I was hoping that part wasn't true."

"Yeah, so was I. And I was really hoping that information hadn't gotten around town."

"Oh, my."

A noise made them turn to see JoAnn, their ten-year-old daughter, standing at the entrance to the room. "So she was murdered? An honest to goodness murder? In Summerfield?" There was a touch of sadness, but more than a little bit of excitement in her voice. "People were talking about Mrs. Mathison's body on the roof after school, but they didn't know she was murdered!"

Pierson closed his eyes for a moment, then opened them again. "Jo, you might as well come in. It seems there aren't any secrets around here." He looked from one to the other. "Look. An investigation is ongoing, which means I can't give any details about what we're doing or what we're finding out till we're done. That's all confidential. Are we clear on that?"

They both nodded.

"My hours may be different for awhile, but you've known that to happen before when we've had a case of some sort. Yes, this is a suspicious death, but we are going to do everything we can to resolve this. And that is all you can tell anybody." He looked particularly at his daughter. "Jo? Nothing about murder. We don't really know what happened. She has died, and we are investigating. You got that?"

"I got it, Dad." She grimaced as if in disappointment, but slowly nodded.

"Alright. Now, if you don't mind, I've got to do some mental sorting out. It's Hazy's night to take any emergency calls, so I'm then going to get some sleep while I can." He got up and left the room, but stopped just outside the door to listen for a minute.

Judy and Jo looked at each other.

"Look," Judy said, "We'll leave Dad alone to deal with this and not bug him. He'll share with us when he can. But, meanwhile, if either of us hears anything, we'll tell each other. Okay?"

Jo nodded. "I'm sorry Mrs. Mathison is dead, but I have to tell you this is the most exciting thing that has happened in Summerfield since, well, since anything that I can remember."

Pierson shook his head, recognizing that this was going to be true for a lot of the town's residents.

# CHAPTER 9

The Summerfield Police Department reconvened in Room A. This morning was unusually quiet, no one joking, and, for the second time in Pierson's memory and in just two days, everyone was on time for a meeting, even George Peabody, who usually said he couldn't remember where they were supposed to meet. The seriousness of Mrs. Mathison's death apparently had hit home.

Doughnuts and hot drinks had been provided by Marie Hazlett, as befitted her motherly approach to the department, a habit that no one had ever really tried to break her of, since it worked to everybody else's advantage. She checked briefly with Pierson, who asked her to use her contacts around town to see if there was any information in Grace Mathison's background that could suggest anything, anything at all, and also to check with Harry Townsend's previous employment... "Ask Sherri Northrup for contact information." She then left to man the phones or the front door or whatever needed manning. Joining the team around the table, at least briefly, were Phil Culbertson from the crime scene unit and Mayor Jonathan "JJ" Plummer.

Pierson turned from the chalkboard where he had been adding notes from his interview the previous evening and faced the other officers.

"Good morning, all. I hope you got a good night's rest. You'll need it." He pointed to their guests. "Phil will be providing us with whatever his crime scene techs found yesterday. And JJ is here, well, I guess, to represent the village of Summerfield. JJ?"

"Jeff." Plummer stood and nodded to each person in turn. "Steph, Bud, George, Phil. I am not here to intrude on the investigation. And I am certainly not here to put pressure on anyone. But, as the duly elected representative for Summerfield, I do get phone calls from the press, both

Paul Cousins at *The Summerfield Weekly*, and Beth Goodkind, the crime reporter at *The Oldstown Press*." Everybody was familiar with the daily newspaper from the neighboring big city. "Also from the town council and other leading citizens representing this fine community. I have a duty and a responsibility to keep them updated on our police department's progress. I do wish to express and confirm my utter faith in each and every one of you."

Peabody muttered to no one in particular, but to everyone in general, "You're already elected, JJ."

Plummer paused. "What was that, George?"

"Nothing, JJ, nothing, just clearing my throat. At my age, I have to do that a lot." And he demonstrated.

"Fine, thank you, George. We all understand that. So I am here just so I can assure the good folks of our town that we are actively and fervently pursuing all avenues to solve this terrible crime as soon as possible."

Pierson passed the piece of chalk from one hand to another, back and forth. "Thank you, JJ. We do appreciate your words of support. You can inform anyone that asks that all we have at this point is a suspicious death and that we are currently investigating all avenues. I think we want to be very careful with the terms we use. All of us were busy yesterday following up on leads and interviewing various interested members of the community. You can also share that information. I expect you'll hear back from some of the people we interviewed yourself. At this time, I don't believe we have any specific people of interest that we can mention for the record." He looked around at his staff, and not getting any disagreement, continued, "We're going to hear what Phil has to tell us, and the results of the interviews, then determine what our next steps are.

"JJ, I do understand your position, so when we have anything concrete, you will be the first to know. I imagine, as mayor and with your law practice, you already have a busy day ahead of you, so, if you want, you can go back to your law office, and I'll keep in touch with you."

Plummer nodded solemnly to everybody again, grabbed one, no, two doughnuts, and one of the coffees, and left. His office, Plummer and Whittlesey, Attorneys At Law, was directly across the green, making it a short walk from one job to the next, and then back again.

"Phil, what have you got for us?" Pierson nodded to Culbertson.

Culbertson didn't stand, but did, momentarily, put down his bagel.

"Gentlemen...and lady," he added. "We have bupkis on the murder weapon." Pierson cringed again slightly at the official use of the word murder. "Nothing on the roof but her blood, and not much at that, and nothing on the ground below, anywhere around the house. We did find some of what appears to be blood mixed in with the mud at the foot of the ladder, and we're getting that analyzed. But the ladder was washed clean by the rain. And because of the rain and the mud, and all the people trampling everywhere, the yard was pretty chewed up by the time we got to it, but we found no rock or any other object that could have caused that particularly round-shaped blow to her head. It was wet under where her body had been, but not as much as the rest of the roof, so our conclusion is that Mrs. Mathison was placed there during the storm, not before or after. That makes the time of death somewhere between ten PM and four AM."

"However," his tone became more serious, "inside the house, we did find some blood traces to the left of the mantel, and in a splatter pattern consistent with a blow to the left temple. It looks like there was an attempt to clean some of it up, and it wouldn't have been really noticeable if we hadn't been looking for it, but the bet is that's where she was killed. We're having tests to match it up with Mrs. Mathison, but, unless there was a very violent altercation, and there's no physical evidence of that, the odds are it is hers. We're also checking for fingerprints besides hers, but I know at least three of you were in there and who knows who else visited her. Probably not tons of people, but she wasn't a recluse either. We'd need prints on the murder weapon to match up anyway, and there's no sign of anything like that yet."

Reasoner interrupted. "What about the two glasses on the sink?"

"Fingerprints on only one of them, the one Jeff apparently picked up, which is a little odd. You would expect something from her. But they were freshly washed and apparently left to air-dry. So maybe she was very particular in her washing."

"And used the washcloth to place them upside down on the counter?" Reasoner again.

Culbertson shrugged. "That's why I said you would expect some prints, at least partials. It is strange that there are none."

"You have been thorough, Phil," Pierson commented.

"You may not get much in the way of serious crime here, but we do get a few homicides in Oldstown. We've had the practice, and we do know what we're doing." He tapped an envelope on the table in front of him. "There are some pictures for you, both outside and in the house, and of the particular areas and locations Bud asked for. You will get my written report later today."

He picked up the bagel and took a bite. "I do hate to say it, but I don't think forensics is going to solve this case. This is probably going to take legwork, witnesses, and good old-fashioned deductions. Motive, opportunity, and means. MOM, as I like to call it."

Peabody raised his hand. "Do you have anything for POPS?"

Everybody chuckled but Culbertson.

"Perpetrator Outcome – Prison Sentence. Why?"

That got a slightly louder chuckle and a grin from Peabody.

Pierson stood and turned to the chalkboard. Hazlett had rewritten everything from the day before in her neat, legible printing, leaving plenty of room for additional columns and information.

"Thanks, Phil." He added columns for WHO, WHY, HOW and, after pausing to think, TUES NIGHT. "That will be for whereabouts. We'll go through what we've got and fill in these as much as we can, then figure out what we need to get and where we need to go from this point. Of course, the biggest questions will be to think of WHOs to start with. There's not a lot of likely suspects yet. Which, I admit, is not what you would expect at this point, but everybody, and I mean everybody, genuinely seemed to like her."

He turned to Culbertson. "Phil, you have anything else?" At the shake of his head, Pierson continued. "You're welcome to stay. You've got more experience than any of us, but I know your end is the crime scene forensics."

"I need to get back. I'll be the one to cover your case, but Oldstown had a drug shootout last night, two dead so far and two in the hospital, and many of the others from our unit will be involved in that, so I need to be the one to get your stuff done." He took the last bite from his bagel and stood up. "I'll leave the rest of these for you. We've got our own goodies in the lab right next to the blood samples." He winked in the direction of Reasoner, but got no response, and left.

"Okay, people, what do we have?" Pierson tossed his chalk from one hand to the other. "Pops? Anything that can help clear up the muddied waters?"

Peabody reported on his interviews with the neighbors, lightly touching on the snacks, but concluded with, "The only thing of significance was Miss Bucholtz seeing that car in the driveway. Nobody else was looking outside during the rain. Or had any reason to. The gray sedan, four-door, with five characters on the license plate and the round sticker in the back window, though I'm not sure if she really could tell that. That's not a lot to go on."

"Almost like my family car," said Pierson, "and Hazy's and a few hundred others, probably." He wrote it specifically under the miscellaneous clues column, and "unknown car" under WHO.

Peabody shrugged. "Well, Hazy's is more of a dusty black."

"Not in the rain," said Reasoner. "Then it's less dusty."

Pierson turned toward her. "Speed, what can you give us?"

"I checked on Harry Townsend's alibi as soon as I left his office. This Missy Walters did confirm it. She wasn't uncomfortable about it, and it didn't sound rehearsed or planned. She expressed what appeared to be appropriate regret at his aunt's death and gave details regarding their night together." Peabody's eyebrows rose. "Much more than I wanted to know. And a restaurant confirms them having dinner together in New Lincoln, which is about an hour away. At this point, it does appear that Townsend was where everybody thought he was. But..."

"'But', Speed?" Pierson prompted.

Reasoner hesitated. "But he was only an hour away, and he might have been able to leave and get back while she was sleeping. Maybe not likely, but he could have.

"Meanwhile nobody is aware of any outstanding debts on his part, and he does seem to be successful enough in the insurance business to maintain his current lifestyle legitimately. Everyone reports the relationship between him and Mrs. Mathison as loving with no obvious major conflicts."

Pierson wrote "Harry Townsend" under WHO and noted his whereabouts under TUES NIGHT, as well as "Inheritance" with a question mark, under WHY.

"I'm going to put him down even though he appears to have an alibi for that time. But we're ruling out as well as narrowing in. Anybody have any idea what kind of car he drives?"

Reasoner responded. "A two-door Honda Civic, bright red. I asked Sherri, then checked in their parking lot."

"Okay. Good job, Speed. Anything else right now?"

She shrugged. "I don't know what kind of car Missy Walters drives. He might have been able to borrow it without her knowing. Other than that, nothing at the moment."

"Alright. Bud?"

Addams gave a room-by-room report, noting the two glasses on the kitchen sink and the apparently random collection of odd knickknacks. In the basement, he had also found several boxes of the same miscellaneous… junk, for lack of a better word.

"The only indications of anything missing were the few things from the living room cabinet that didn't match up with the picture. I didn't notice any other blank areas, but then there was so much stuff it's hard to tell. And there could be whole boxes missing, and we'd have no way of knowing. We can check with Harry Townsend if he knows about the values of any of her stuff and can get us into a safety deposit box, but, without digging deep into any drawers or cabinets, I couldn't find any list of a specific collection."

Peabody put down his second cinnamon roll and interjected, "I hate to add any unnecessary work, but we could also see if she liked to frequent garage sales or auctions. Sometimes they sell stuff by the boxful, and you don't always know what you're getting. My wife likes to go to those types of things, just to see what might show up. I think that's half our house now. At least I don't know where much of our stuff came from. I know I didn't buy most of it."

"I get that, that's not a bad idea," Addams responded. "But why then display all of them? I would think you'd pick out what you want, then just put the rest out for another sale, or even pitch them."

Reasoner spoke up. "Speaking of garage sales, didn't we have some recent reports within the last six months of thefts at garage, yard, and tag sales, with all sorts of things being taken? Small appliances and electronics, but also odd boxes of collectibles and assorted – junk." She turned to Pierson. "It appeared to be that someone was checking out homes and valuables while visiting these sales. Somewhere we should have lists of what was taken. Jeff, you had that happen, didn't you?"

Rolling his eyes, Pierson reluctantly replied, "Yeah, we did. It's hard to admit that the police chief was robbed, particularly when I was right there. I didn't even want to report it, but I think Judy made up a list of what she thought was taken -- stuff that she was sure she put out but had no specific record that it was sold. And she was meticulous in keeping track of what was there and what went. I didn't get to pick what was going to go into the sale and what wasn't, so I really have no idea what was out there to take. I do think we had an old microwave and a stereo system that disappeared."

"Was Grace Mathison there?" Addams asked.

"I don't know. I was in and out of the house a lot. There was a ballgame on the TV that I wanted to watch, and Judy ran the sale. Our agreement was that she sell what she wanted and I stayed out of it." He grimaced. "But I can't imagine Mrs. Mathison walking out with the microwave and stereo. I don't remember seeing her there, and I just can't see her doing anything like that."

"Those bigger articles aren't the same types of things we're talking about in her house, and that doesn't explain her death," Addams added. "Even if some of her collection ends up being some of the same smaller objects that are reported stolen."

"But it gives us a place to start." Reasoner took a sip from her coffee. "Maybe we should check if she had a history of doing anything like that. You know, picking up small things from people's homes, or from the school."

Pierson tapped his chalk on the board. "I asked Hazy to check on some background for both her and Townsend. I'll ask her to be more specific in her questions, particularly in regards to that."

Addams pulled the envelope that Culbertson had brought over to him. "I did request Phil to take pictures of the various boxes and cabinets, and to blow up the photo of the cabinet from before so we can see exactly what isn't there anymore."

"You take a look at that, Bud." Pierson wrote "garage sale thefts" under his initial column of general comments, then, after a pause, added it to the WHY column with a big question mark. There were as many question marks as any other comments on the board.

"Meanwhile, it seems to be stretching it to tie it to this case, but I'll note it. Anything else to add to our board? Any other WHOs?" He turned back to the team. "Not so much so far. Especially with Harry seemingly unlikely as a suspect."

Reasoner pointed at the board. "You talked with Mel Johnson. I admit it's very improbable, but you should put his name down. And maybe jealousy or frustration as a motive if she didn't reciprocate his feelings."

Pierson sighed and reluctantly added that information. "I really didn't get any sense that, at his age, he was going to get that upset about any of his feelings getting hurt. I think he'd be more worried about what other people would think if he did something about it. He seemed to be okay with where their relationship was, and to be aware it was unlikely to lead to marriage. And I can't see him carrying her up to the roof."

"That seems to be an issue all the way around," Peabody commented. "Who would have been strong enough to get her to the roof, and why? What was the point? I haven't even been up on my roof in years."

"But," Reasoner noted. "Various people were up on her roof. Regularly. To get her cat. It's an excuse for her to be up there. He, I hate to say it, but it's probably a 'he', would have wanted us to assume, like most of us first did, that she had slipped and fallen and died from exposure."

Pierson caught the "most of us", but didn't comment on the remark. He turned back to Addams. "Anything else, Bud?"

Addams, just starting to look through the pictures from the envelope, shook his head.

"Okay. What we've got so far is an unidentified car in the driveway, maybe around the time of death, but not sure, no real suspects, and unexplained 'junk' in her house, that may, or probably may not, have anything to do with her death. Not a lot to go on, is there?"

Addams found a picture and held it up. "I'd like to go through the lists of stolen goods from the garage sales and anywhere else and see if I can match it up with anything in her house." He shook his head. "It is such an odd collection that I don't know how else to explain it."

"Sure, why not. Maybe that would solve one mystery anyway. Pops, why don't you check with her friends to see if they know anything about her collection or any disagreements with anyone? Hazy will probably know at least some of the members of her book club. Speed, talk with Harry Townsend about any possible valuables in the house and see if you and he can get into a safety deposit box, if she has one."

"Jeff, I'm not real comfortable being alone with him." Reasoner spun her coffee cup in her hands. "I always feel like he's … checking me out, if you know what I mean. It's uncomfortable anyway, but now, with his aunt having died, it's downright creepy."

"Yeah, I can appreciate that, Speed, and I don't want you to be in a situation that could get awkward at the least." Pierson considered what she was saying for a moment. "I don't want to seem like a jerk here, but has he actually said or done anything? Or is it more of a sense that he might?"

"He hasn't done anything, and it's not that I really think he's going to, but, I just don't know." She straightened up. "I can do it. Forget I said anything. Nothing's going to happen."

"The thing is you've already met with him, and I think he's comfortable with you, and he may tell you some things he wouldn't tell anyone else. You're a professional, but, if there's any real problem, let me know. Okay?"

She nodded, not too happily, but seeming to recognize the priority.

Pierson continued, "I think we had a good discussion this morning. I like this kind of interaction among us. But we don't really have much yet, so we've got a lot of work to do. Let's get to it."

As they started to gather up notes, he looked at his watch. "Let's meet at…four o'clock, that okay?" They all nodded. "Unless you've found something that we need to know right away. Then get Marie to gather us all together."

Addams and Peabody went to talk with Hazlett regarding the list of stolen items and the names of the book club members, while Reasoner reluctantly but dutifully left for another meeting with Harry Townsend.

Pierson went into his office, shut the door, and sat down to think. It was a real mess so far, with no clear answers yet, but some information was entering the picture that needed thoughtful and quiet consideration.

He was still there a half hour later, sitting with his head in his hands when Hazlett knocked. He said "Yeah?" and she opened the door.

"Jeff, I hate to bring this up at this time, but it's bowling league tonight. I'm going to call and see if I can get us rescheduled, but I don't know for when."

"No, Hazy. I can't be there, not unless somebody walks in and confesses today, preferably before lunch. But you and JJ and Paul go. See if Roy Washington can take my place. He's a high school teacher; he certainly doesn't have anything to do with this. I know he's not as good as me," Pierson shrugged and ruefully grinned, "but he's better than a forfeit."

"Are you sure?"

"Hazy, you need the night out. You had watch last night. I know it's Bud's turn to be available and take any calls, but I also know I'll just be hanging around here for a while and trying to figure this out. Speed and Pops have the next two nights, but I suspect I will be having late nights too until this thing gets resolved. That's what I supposedly get paid to do, to take the worry and responsibility. Hopefully the others will come up with new information, and maybe something will click. I think I'm pretty much on this until we come up with the answer, or the town council selects another police chief. Whichever comes first."

# CHAPTER 10

Following the department meeting, Reasoner slowly made her way back down the street to interview Harry Townsend. As she passed the green one more time, she detoured to the bandstand and sat down on the steps. There were lights on at the Johnson & Johnson Insurance office, but she wanted a few moments to gather her thoughts and decide just what information she specifically wanted before approaching Townsend again.

She had always liked this spot. Downtown Summerfield presented itself in front of her, with the shops and businesses vital to the town's life just starting their mornings. She saw movement in some windows and a few mid-morning shoppers or late-arriving workers on the sidewalks. Hank Peters was setting up a display outside his hardware store. The head of the town council, Myron Stump, liked to take his morning constitutional around the green, checking that "his" town was in good shape before heading to his furniture-making shop two blocks away at the northernmost end of the green. The day lay ahead of them, with all sorts of possibilities and dreams. It wasn't the chaos and the noise and the stress of the big city, but it was life nonetheless. People grew up here, and had families here, and lived their complete lives here, with joy and satisfaction and no regrets.

But now a murder. An actual police case. Something to be solved rather than just processed. Something to raise the adrenaline.

If Harry Townsend, the most legitimate suspect, the only one with even the glimmer of a motive, had an alibi, then that left the field either wide open or closed shut. A motive had to be found, and one of the biggest questions in this case other than who? was why? Why would anybody want to harm, not to mention kill, Grace Mathison? That was the first thing everybody said when they heard the news – why kill Grace Mathison? No one had an answer for that question, could even suggest a possibility to answer it.

Reasoner thought back over what just passed through her mind. Not why kill Grace, but the word "harm", why harm her? And go back even further. Maybe, just maybe, there wasn't even an intent to harm. Bud said several objects seemed to be missing from her bric-a-brac shelves and Culbertson had found blood near those shelves. Maybe this whole incident had been a spur of the moment thing, closer to the idea of an accident, like Harry Townsend earlier insisted. The perpetrator had picked up something from the shelf and swung it in ... anger? Frustration? Fear? Guilt?

So maybe the motive they should be looking for was not why kill her, but why try to cover it up? Why not call an ambulance, try to get help? Perhaps it did have to do with the missing – junk after all.

It had to be someone strong enough to carry her up to the roof. The roof is still an odd place for the body to be, but someone had to get her up there. That should rule out most, probably all of her teacher friends and book club members. If they were around her age, no one could carry her, certainly not that far. And Mel Johnson was even a few years older, and reportedly wasn't in that great of health. It had been a surprise to the community when his wife had died first.

That brought it back around to Harry. Young and strong enough. Reasons to be in her house with her. But he had the alibi.

In the movies, or even in a television show, Reasoner could break down Missy Walters' alibi for him, but this wasn't a TV show. Reasoner had talked with her and really had the sense that Missy was telling the truth, that Harry was with her that night. Apparently all night.

So who did that leave? Well, that's why there was a police department and why they were interviewing people and investigating scenes. To find out those answers. Somewhere there was an answer to the who and an answer to why.

She stood up and dusted herself off. It was time to get back to Harry. That might not answer *who*, but it could address the *why*.

# CHAPTER 11

"Hey, Sherri," Reasoner said as she entered the insurance office. Sherri Northrup smiled up at the interruption of her routine. The police officer wanted to keep the interaction brief, but Sherri, apparently sometimes bored with continually sitting behind her desk and always ready to talk, didn't really know the meaning of the word.

"Oh, hi, Steph. How are you doing today? Do you have any suspects yet? I heard that it was murder, can you believe it? In Summerfield? To Mrs. Mathison? Who would want to do that? She was such a nice person. At least that's what everyone says, but you never know, do you?" Without waiting for any answers or seeming to take a breath, she continued, "Who did you want to see? Mel and Harry both went over to his aunt's house. Harry wanted to look around. And Mel went just for somebody to be with him, you know. I wanted to go too, but they said to stay here and look after the office. As if the clients come to see me. I can't tell them much of anything."

Reasoner straightened up. "He's not supposed to be there at the house. He won't be allowed inside. I think the department hired the former police chief, Mike Wannamaker, the one before Jeff, to stay there and make sure no one entered the property, because it's now a crime scene."

"Oh, I don't think Harry knew that he wasn't supposed to go there. He figured it's his aunt's house. Or it was, and now it's probably really his. So he just wanted to look at it. You can understand that, can't you?"

Reasoner nodded. "Yeah, I can. But he's still not supposed to be there, particularly unescorted. How long ago did he leave?"

"Maybe half an hour? He was here, but wasn't getting anything done, could he, thinking about his aunt? So he's probably still there. You could wait, but I don't know when they'll be back. I don't think he'll be able to settle down till this is figured out. I know I can't." She almost took a breath, "Isn't it a shame?"

"Thanks, Sherri, I think I'll try and find him there." She turned toward the door.

"If you change your mind about waiting, there are a couple of good magazines here. I think the Cosmo is only three months old."

The door closed behind Reasoner before she could hear about the ages of any other periodicals.

—  —  —

She found Harry Townsend and Mel Johnson in the front yard of his aunt's house, talking with Mike Wannamaker. Wannamaker was sitting in a folding lawn chair with a newspaper across his lap and a thermos at his feet. Apparently standing at the front door looking menacing was not going to be his style.

"Mike." She nodded as she approached. Though she had not known him as the chief, it was hard not to be familiar with Mike Wannamaker through the relationships he had developed throughout his time. And he still liked to stop into the police station now and then for whatever reason he could make up.

"Steph." Wannamaker smiled. "Mr. Townsend here told me he wanted to see inside and I told him no. He asked for how long, and I told him that wasn't up to me. We were just discussing what the word no meant."

"Steph." Townsend also smiled at her, seemingly hoping a hint of personal charm and the use of a first name would work on somebody. Johnson held out his hand, and she took it.

"Mr. Townsend, Mr. Johnson." She was determined to keep this interaction professional. "It's still considered an active crime scene. I do realize your personal interest, but I'm sure you understand."

"I just wanted to make sure everything was still okay. And..." Townsend pointed with his whole hand at the house, "...maybe, just maybe, I could tell if something had been taken. You know, maybe something of value. And that would possibly give us a reason for this whole thing. Maybe?"

Reasoner had to admit to herself that he had a point. They had the pictures that showed some small trinkets missing, but he didn't know that, and there was a legitimate possibility that there was something of real worth that they simply didn't know about. That was one of the questions she was here to ask him, and, well, yes, going inside the house could be the best way to find out.

"Give me a moment." She stepped a short distance away, pulling the radio from her belt. After a short conversation, she came back to the group. "Tell you what. I just talked with the chief. We'll go through the house together, room by room. You can let me know what's supposed to be where, and if something is missing." She turned to Wannamaker. "That okay with you, Mike?"

Wannamaker shrugged. "Works for me. I'll just keep sitting here and make sure you're not disturbed."

Townsend didn't look as happy as she thought he should. He was getting what he wanted, but it appeared that he'd rather have done it by himself. Johnson touched him on the arm.

"Harry, we just want to see the house. Officer Reasoner's suggestion sounds good. I'll go with you too."

"Yeah, we can do that." The smile came back, but not as naturally, as if he had to consciously will it back.

"Just remember this is a crime scene, so don't touch anything," Reasoner said. "And, not to be insensitive, but this is where your aunt died. It may upset you."

Townsend took a deep breath. "Yeah, I realize that. But I'm going to have to go in there sometime. It might as well be now."

Reasoner led the way to the front door and bent under the "Do Not Disturb - Police" tape.

They were now basically in the middle of the house. Reasoner turned left toward the living room and the apparent scene of the crime, but Townsend started straight down the hall toward the bedrooms.

"Mr. Townsend, let's start in the kitchen. The ladder was beside the back door, and these are the rooms where we have found some things that I'd like to ask you about."

He paused and looked toward the hall to the bedrooms, then turned and followed Reasoner. Johnson trailed behind. "Of course. You lead the way, Officer. I will go where thou takest me."

"Yes, you will." Reasoner had to work at not rolling her eyes. "And remember, don't touch anything."

"Well, my fingerprints are probably over everything anyway. You know, I have been here a lot."

"Mr. Townsend, It's not just the fingerprints. We're trying to preserve things as they were at the time of the – incident."

"I understand. I will touch only what you let me touch. They tell me I am good at following directions. Lead the way."

As they passed through the living room, she kept her eyes on him, looking for a reaction, but he never glanced at the knick-knack cabinet or the floor where the crime scene unit found blood. When he saw that she was watching him, he raised his eyebrows in a question, but she merely continued into the kitchen and pointed at the glasses on the sink.

"Sir, you mentioned it being unusual for her to have two glasses on the sink. Already washed."

Townsend took a step towards the sink and gestured toward the glasses. "Those are glasses she would have gotten out for a guest." Johnson nodded in confirmation. "The one she would have used by herself during the day would usually have been smaller. Starting out for just juice in the morning. These are dinner glasses or for guests." He looked up at Reasoner. "But then, I wasn't here all the time. There may have been a reason for two glasses, or she just wanted to do something different. It's odd for her, but I really couldn't tell you if it's significant."

"If it was unusual, it may be telling us that she was on friendly terms with whoever killed her. That goes along with no forced entry. That she had invited whomever in and to have a drink with her. Would she have washed the glasses immediately?"

"No, that would have waited till they were gone, maybe even the next morning. She wasn't that much of a cleaning nut. She would have wanted more dishes to do at one time."

"Do you see anything else out of order in the kitchen? Anything missing or out of place?"

Townsend looked around. "Well, again, I wouldn't know where everything is, but nothing hits me as specifically different. Do you mind if

I open the cupboards?"

Reasoner paused then nodded. The crime scene unit had already been here, so he couldn't mess things up too badly. "Go ahead."

"I can't imagine there would have been anything of value in any of these, but she did once tell me she kept a few dollars in an old tea box. Thought she was being different than using an old coffee can. Let's see." Reaching up he pushed a few cans aside. "Ah, here it is."

Before Reasoner could stop him, he pulled down what was labeled as iced tea bags, but, when opened, the box turned out to be filled with twenty-dollar bills. Quite a few of them.

"Whoa, looks like more than enough for a rainy day." He whistled.

Reasoner pulled a cloth out of her back pocket so that she wouldn't be directly handling the evidence any more than she needed to. Johnson offered her his handkerchief, but she shook her head and took the box from Townsend, holding it gingerly by the edges.

"Who else would have known about this?"

"Maybe Mel." But Johnson shook his head. "Looking at it, I can't imagine anything missing. It's absolutely stuffed. I had no idea she had that much in there – anybody could have taken most of it, and no one would ever have known." He grabbed another box and opened it. It too was full of money. "Maybe she didn't believe in banks."

Reasoner looked up at that. "Really?"

But Townsend shook his head. "No, I know she had an account. I don't know how much is in it, but I did take her to the bank at times. I was just being facetious."

"Mr. Townsend, I think we need to leave these alone for now. I will notify our crime scene people to look through the boxes in these cupboards more closely.

"But it also tells us the attack was apparently not done by someone looking for money. This was not the best hiding place, but it served its purpose. The money is still here." Reasoner pointed at the floor. "The floor was wet in spots when we first came in yesterday morning, but that was probably the perpetrator." She almost said 'killer' in front of him. "Returning to wash the glasses and – whatever."

They moved into the living room. Again she watched his eyes, but they did not go to one spot right away. Townsend's eyes seemed to be wandering, trying to take in everything. They did finally pause at the cabinet.

"That cabinet seems to be different, but I couldn't tell you what was different about it. I never paid that much attention to it. To be honest, it was all junk to me. Aunt Grace liked all that stuff, but I didn't see any value in any of it. I don't think she had anything of any real value. Not being a dealer in those things, maybe there was something there, but I wouldn't know it. And neither would she. To her, her possessions were of sentimental value only. I asked her about specific insurance for anything valuable, but she just wanted general for house and contents."

Johnson agreed. "I'm not aware of any specific items that she referred to as being valuable or as being particularly meaningful. Outside of objects that prompted memories of her marriage to Ralph."

"Do you know where she got these?"

Townsend's mouth tightened briefly, but then he shrugged. "I assume they were gifts or souvenirs she had picked up someplace. As I said, I never paid much attention to them. I used to bring her a few things from trips or where I used to live, but they were just personal souvenirs."

"She has a lot of this stuff." Reasoner walked over to the cabinet. "Why would she have this golf trophy? We didn't find any golf clubs. She wasn't a golfer, was she?"

Townsend looked puzzled. "No, she wasn't. Maybe Uncle Ralph when he was younger, but I don't remember it."

"It says three years ago. It wouldn't have been Ralph's, because he died before that. Do you golf?"

He slowly shook his head. Johnson said, "I do, but I never won any trophies."

"And a basketball one from two years ago." Reasoner looked up at Townsend. "Was she ever involved in any of the local basketball leagues, in any capacity?"

He shook his head. "I, I don't know where those came from."

"Or why she would have them?"

"Or why she would have them. I never looked closely at them. I just knew she had them."

"And on the mantel." She pointed at the fireplace. "And in the other rooms. There are shelves full of them throughout the house. There was a box of toy soldiers in the hall closet. Not the type of things you would expect Mrs. Mathison to have."

"No, they're not. And I can tell you the toy soldiers weren't mine."

"And you're not aware of anything missing?"

"Not specifically. I just know that those shelves," he said, pointing again to the cabinet, "seem less full than before."

"We found a picture of the two of you in this room that shows the cabinet to the side, and we've identified some things that are not there now."

Reasoner pulled the picture from a pocket. "It's one of the reasons I was coming to see you today. To ask if you were aware of any special significance to them."

She showed him the picture. "We have identified a bowling trophy, a small bowl, a toy train engine, and a small statuette of two figures, as well as a couple of miscellaneous vague items. Did she bowl?"

Townsend studied the picture for a moment then shook his head. "Not that I know of. Not for several years anyway. I think she used to take her elementary class for a bowling night, but there wouldn't have been any trophy involved. Certainly not for her. Now that you mention it, I do recall seeing the Laurel and Hardy figure, but I never thought anything of it. I just assumed she or Uncle Ralph was a fan. Probably Ralph. I never heard her refer to them at all."

Reasoner turned to Mel Johnson. "Did you and she ever bowl, Mr. Johnson?"

He looked up from the picture. "No. No, I suggested it once, but she said she had a weak wrist and the balls were too heavy. So I didn't bring it up again. We didn't do anything involving physical exercise. Well, sports anyway."

Reasoner ignored the last remark and took the picture back. "Again, nothing particular to her interests. But apparently of interest to somebody. Thank you for confirming the Laurel and Hardy. We weren't quite sure."

She indicated the spot on the floor between the cabinet and the fireplace. She initially wasn't going to point it out, but thought she'd never get another chance to get his first reaction.

"This is where they found blood. Someone tried to clean it up, but they didn't get it all."

"Oh my God." Townsend put his hand to his mouth. "They think she was killed here?"

To her admittedly untrained eye, the reaction appeared genuine. She noted that Johnson had turned away and was leaving the room. She began to call after him, but he had already gone before she could get the words out, so she turned back to Townsend.

"Nothing is certain, but it appears likely."

He involuntarily took a step back. "I didn't realize...I didn't think...hell, I should have asked first. I'm sorry, it just took me...a little bit bigger shock than I expected."

He turned toward the hallway. "Can we go somewhere else? Or is there something else here that I should know about?"

"No, no, nothing else like that. We'll go take a look at some of the other rooms now."

The two of them first descended the basement steps. She heard a toilet flush upstairs, telling her where Johnson had gone. Five boxes containing the same sort of curios as the cabinets did upstairs, but Townsend could not tell her anything new. Nothing that he would have associated with his aunt and nothing worth anything except as a keepsake.

Johnson was waiting for them at the top of the steps. "I'm sorry, I, I wasn't expecting that reaction."

Reasoner decided she didn't really want to hear about the exact nature of his reaction and led them to the master bedroom, where Addams had found the picture of Grace Mathison and her nephew.

Townsend entered reluctantly. "I was never in here. Well, almost never. After Ralph's death, she had me in here once to see if there were any clothes that I wanted. We were not the same size, but I think she wanted to offer. I took a couple of ties and tie pins, but I don't know if I've ever even used them."

"There are a couple of jewelry boxes." Reasoner pointed. "Would you know anything about her jewelry, either of you?"

"Not enough to help you. The only pieces I was familiar with were a black pearl necklace that Uncle Ralph gave her and her diamond engagement ring that she always wore." Townsend looked at her and Reasoner nodded.

"She still had it when we found her." Reasoner opened one of the boxes. "And the necklace is here on top."

Johnson added. "I only knew that she wore jewelry, but I never bought her any. She said she had all she wanted, and I never really paid any attention to that sort of thing, even what my own wife wore. Those pieces do look like what Grace wore, but I can't tell you anything else."

Townsend opened the other box without asking. "Some of this looks familiar, but only now that I see it. Again, I think the only value is sentimental. She was not big into expensive jewelry. I got her a bracelet once for her birthday, but I think she only wore it a couple of times and then just to let me know that she would wear it." He moved a couple of pieces with the tip of a finger. "Here it is. No one took that."

They closed the boxes and moved across the hall. This apparently was her hobby room and office. The table with the sewing machine and fabrics took up most of the area with a small desk against the right wall.

"Aunt Grace did like to sew. Her specialty was those blankets or quilts with personal designs or remnants such as T-shirts on them. She liked to give them as gifts – I have two of them, but I believe she also did some orders for friends. You know, like for a grandchild with all their soccer team shirts on it. Or something with all twelve grandchildren names. That sort of thing. One of mine had all my schools and logos and the other was some personal interests."

Johnson said, "And I had one with my different organizations and clubs. It was a Christmas present one year."

Reasoner looked down at the papers on the desk. "You ever help her with her bills?"

Townsend shook his head. "She showed me her system once. A pile with due dates to the left. Stamps, envelopes, and return address labels on the shelf above. Her checkbook in the middle and a manila envelope for major receipts to the right. Not complicated. She had few big bills. The house and the car were paid off."

Reasoner picked up the checkbook and leafed through the last several pages. Gas, utilities, groceries, nothing jumped out at her. She handed it to

Townsend.

"Anything strike you as out of line, as unusual?"

He went more slowly through the last ten pages. "No, I don't know the usual monthly bills, but these seem to be fairly typical amounts. And I don't know what she would have been buying in these stores, but they seem to be the stores she would usually have shopped at."

Reasoner pulled open the drawers, but it was pencils, pens, paper, extra sets of checks, paper clips, and a stapler. Nothing out of the ordinary.

She did fish out a small red envelope with a bank name on it. "This her safety deposit key?"

"Could be. I have an envelope that looks like that holding my key."

She held it up. "Are you up to looking in it? Maybe she kept something there that no one knows about."

He shrugged. "I wouldn't know what that could be. But then I guess that's the point. Are they going to let me see in it?"

"If I'm with you, there shouldn't be a problem. By now, everyone knows she's deceased, but I'll be your authority."

"Okay, how about when we're done here?'

"Fine." Reasoner pocketed the small envelope.

There was a closet, but it held more fabrics and fashion design plans. Also what appeared to be spare linens. She knew that the crime scene people had been through everything, so there wouldn't be any surprises, although they had just found the tea boxes of money, but there also wasn't anything for Townsend to tell her about.

Townsend just shrugged when looking in the guest bathroom. "Looks the same to me."

The last room to the left was the smaller spare bedroom. Reasoner was surprised at just how much smaller it seemed. She glanced toward the hobby room.

"I would have expected this to be similar in size to the other room."

"I, I think it just has more stuff in it, with the bed and the dressers and the bookcase. It just looks smaller. And it is a little bit less wide."

"And no back window. Just one to the side of the house. That seems odd. The view would have been out back."

"I don't know why. That's the way it's always been. At least since I've been here."

Johnson shrugged. "She once told me that's the way the house came. She never used this room much, so she didn't really care. I think it was Ralph's private sanctum and he liked it dark and secluded. At least that's what she said." He took out his handkerchief and dabbed at his eyes.

Reasoner walked over to the bookcase and noticed that it was right up against the wall. She grasped a corner and gave it a quick tug. It was heavy and seemed to be fixed to the wall. Maybe that made it a stable place to hold more of Mrs. Mathison's collections.

Townsend hurried to her side. "Don't. You might knock over some of Aunt Grace's stuff. Some of it appears breakable."

She backed up a step. "I won't. Though it appears to be the same kind of miscellaneous whatnots as the living room and the basement. You don't think any of this is valuable, do you?"

"No, no. But we don't want to break anything anyway."

Reasoner cocked her head. Townsend had now inserted himself between her and the bookcase.

"Do you notice anything different with the objects in this case?" She asked him.

"Nope, just looks the same to me."

"Why don't you look at it first?" He had been looking at her when he first answered.

This time he did turn and give it a good look. "I didn't come in here very often, either. But the shelves look pretty full, and I don't see any gaps like in the living room cabinet. No, I don't think there's anything missing." He took her gently by the arm. "Why don't we go back to the living room? Maybe there's something that I missed the first time."

As they went back into the hall, Reasoner looked back at the room. She took a few steps to the hobby room, looked in, then stepped back and looked at the spare bedroom again.

"That definitely looks much smaller. I think I want to come back and measure it another time."

"What for? The size of the rooms can't have anything to do with Aunt Grace's death, for Pete's sake."

"Just curious. It's something different, that doesn't fit. It's going to pester me until I figure it out, that's all."

They moved back to the living room, but both Townsend and Johnson stayed away from the corner with the curio cabinet and the fireplace mantel.

"Well, see anything new?" Reasoner asked.

"No, I just thought, after seeing the other rooms, that something might hit me, but I'm not seeing anything different than before. Just the same gaps on the two shelves that your people already caught."

He tried to smile, but not very successfully. "Why don't we go take a look at her safety deposit box?"

As they came back out the front door, Wannamaker folded down his paper, sticking the pencil for the crossword puzzle behind his right ear. "Everything okay? Learn anything new?"

"Not particularly." Reasoner sighed. "A little more personal info about Mrs. Mathison, but nothing that seems to point to murder." Townsend grimaced at the word. "But, Mike, maybe murder isn't the right word. I'm thinking more and more that this is an accidental death that was intended to look like even more of an accident, that placing the body on the roof was to cover up that someone else had even been here. I'm beginning to wonder if the missing pieces from her curio cabinet are really the key."

She intended her words toward Wannamaker as thinking out loud between colleagues, but he inclined his head in Townsend's direction, and she belatedly caught his meaning.

"I'm sorry, Mr. Townsend, this is just wild speculation on my part. I shouldn't have said anything."

He waved his hand. "That's okay. I understand that's what you need to do at first. But do you really think it could have been just an accident?"

She shook her head. "Please don't go by anything I just said. At this point, we're just considering all possibilities."

Now that Townsend had seen inside the house, he seemed to be anxious to go. She stuck out her hand to shake his hand good-bye, even if just temporarily.

"I appreciate you going through the house with me and giving me some insight. Let me know if there's anything else you can think of, either of you."

"Certainly, Stephanie. Thank you for letting me join you. I, I did not enjoy seeing the area where…Aunt Grace died, but I think I needed to do that. I'll see you at the Summerfield Bank in a few minutes?"

She nodded, and both men walked back to Harry's car sitting at the curb and drove away.

"You were right, Mike. I was thinking out loud, but he didn't need to hear that. Not till we know for sure what happened."

"Well, you could be right about it being an accident. It hasn't made sense to be a murder. Yet – and yet what could have caused an accidental death in that situation either? Nothing really makes sense."

He went back to his crossword. "You don't happen to know a six-letter word for 'enigma', with a 'z' in the middle, do you?"

Reasoner responded, "It will come to you, Mike. I'm sure it will come to you." She walked over to her car, leaving him to his puzzles.

# CHAPTER 12

George Peabody sat at his desk staring at the list of four names given to him by Marie Hazlett. These were the other members of Mrs. Mathison's book club, the Summerfield Literary Society, presumptuously titled by the small group of former teachers.

Knowing he might as well get on with it, he opened his brown bag lunch, took a bite out of his peanut butter and pepper jelly sandwich, and dialed the first number.

Larabeth Nelson answered just as he took the second bite and he had to speak through a full mouth.

"Hewwo, dish ish Shash Pibboddy." He swallowed quickly. "This is George Peabody from the Summerfield Police. Excuse me, I had to finish chewing my sandwich. I had just taken a bite."

"Oh, hello, George. It sounded like one of those pervert calls, and I was trying to make up my mind whether I wanted to listen to more or not. At my age, there aren't too many opportunities."

Peabody got to the point. "Larabeth, I'm calling in regards to Grace Mathison's death."

"Oh, yes." She took a deep breath. "I thought someone might at some time. It has been very upsetting."

"Would you mind answering a few questions?"

"Certainly, but I don't know what I can tell you. None of us were there that evening. We have no idea what happened. We were just talking about that."

"You were just talking about that? Are you together now?"

"Yes, we're all here, even Susan. Did you want to come over and talk with all of us? Or," and she lowered her voice, "do you want to speak with us one at a time? I don't know how these...interrogations go. Is that the right word?"

"It's not an interrogation, Larabeth. I just want to find out some things about Grace. No one thinks any of you had anything to do with this. Talking with all of you at once would be good. Maybe somebody remembers something and that memory jars someone else's memory."

"Come on over. Nellie Chamberlain made a cheesecake, you know, the one that always wins at the county fair, and we'll be here for a while."

Peabody quickly finished his sandwich and banana, took a look at the two store-bought cookies he had left, and decided homemade cheesecake sounded much better as dessert. He put the cookies in his top drawer for later – for emergencies he told himself.

———   ———   ———

Larabeth Nelson opened the door immediately, as if she had been standing behind it. What is this with these teachers and anticipating, he thought. She led him into her dining room, where the others were sitting around finishing up their plates of prize-winning cheesecake. Momentarily, he worried until he saw at the far end of the table that half of it was still sitting in the pan.

Larabeth pulled up a chair for him, and went to fetch another plate and fork. Peabody looked around the table at Nellie Chamberlain of cheesecake fame, Mindy Rhodes, and Susan Peabody, his own wife, who rarely, if ever, made cheesecake. He had been surprised to see her name on the list at first as, if he was being honest with himself, he had forgotten the actual name of the book club that she had joined a few years ago. It was just one of those things that she did when he wasn't around.

Susan leaned over to kiss him on the cheek. "George, how has your morning been?"

"What you'd expect. We have little to go on yet, but don't tell anybody. I'm trying to get some background info here. Find out if there's anything we don't know, so I'm talking to people who knew her. And you're one of them," he added gently to his wife.

He turned to encompass all of them. "Thank you for inviting me over, Larabeth, and for the cheesecake. You especially, Nellie. I'm sure you're all aware of what has happened. It seems everyone in town is. At least to some extent or another."

"That's why Larabeth asked us over, George," Susan interrupted. "We all wanted to pool what we knew and, you know, talk about it."

Peabody nodded in response to all of their heads nodding. "We know she had a cat," he started.

"Reginald." Mindy said. "I have him right now."

"Reginald. And that Reginald frequently got stuck out on the roof."

"All the time," Nellie added.

"Yes, frequently, as I said. Usually, Grace would have called somebody to help, but we haven't heard that she did that two nights ago." No one said anything. "But we do have reason to believe that someone was over that night, whether to rescue the cat or not. Any ideas who that might have been, ladies? Any ideas at all?"

Larabeth shook her head. "None of us," then looked at the others for confirmation.

"It wasn't our book club night, or going to a movie, or out to dinner night." Nellie confirmed. "*Ladies of the Manor* was on PBS that night, and we all have to watch it."

Susan added, "We were, um, doing things together, George, remember?"

"Yes, I, um, remember."

"Do we need an alibi, George?" Mindy sounded concerned. "I live alone, and I wasn't doing things with anyone."

"No, no. You don't need alibis. I know you didn't have book club, but we were hoping someone might have known if Grace was going to have some other guest."

"Grace did sometimes see Mel Johnson, you know," Susan said.

"But I don't think they were doing anything together that night," Larabeth added. "I remember her saying she was expecting to have a quiet week. Her nephew, Harry, was going to be out of town, and she and Mel were going to wait for the Southern Meatloaf Special Night on Fridays at Mac's. It was his favorite. It got him in the mood, if you know what I mean."

"I don't think I need to know what you mean." George looked uncomfortable, but Susan smiled. "We have talked with Mel Johnson.

According to him, they didn't see each other that night. Is there anyone else that she might have had over? Someone that might have just dropped in?"

Nellie spoke up, "She sometimes did talk with Ms. Bucholtz across the street, but I think she always went over there."

"And sometimes some of her neighbors out in the yard," Mindy added. "But only in good weather. And that wasn't that night. Nosiree."

Susan said, "And some people from church. Occasionally. But, as Mindy said, not in that type of weather. Nobody's going to just drop in when it's storming like that. And not that late."

"So it was probably somebody she called over?" Peabody asked. "Or somebody totally unexpected? Anybody know anyone with a gray four-door sedan?"

Both Nellie and Mindy raised their hands and said, "I have one" practically in unison. Then pointed at each other. "And so does she."

Peabody sighed. "Yeah, there appears to be quite a few of them."

He took a couple of bites of cheesecake while they watched him. Nobody said anything until he was done.

"Would you like another piece, George?" Nellie asked. "It won the prize at the county fair, you know?"

"I know, and deservedly so. Ladies, I do have another question," as he held out his plate for the refill. "We have found quite a collection of knick-knacks in her house. With no real pattern to them. Almost as if they had belonged to different households. Many of them don't seem to have any personal connection to her. Any idea what was going on with that?"

"Oh, yes!" Mindy laughed, Nellie smiled, Larabeth looked embarrassed. Susan answered. "Those were her stories."

"Her stories?" Peabody scratched his forehead in confusion.

"Her stories," Larabeth said with a touch of disgust. As the other women looked at her, she added, "I'm sorry. I got more than a little tired of them."

"She used them to tell stories," Susan continued. "When she was still teaching, she sometimes brought some miscellaneous objects in and prompted her students to tell stories about them. Like, say she brought in a toy horseman. Some boy could write a story about what the horseman had done or was going to do. She would bring in a box of these things and let each of the children pick one, then come up with a story. It was her way of inspiring creativity, but also getting the kids to write." She turned to

Larabeth. "That children's author, Nathan Straw, came from her class."

"Yes, I know," Larabeth replied, but her tone hadn't changed. "And that was fine for her students, but she kept doing it after she had retired. Only she was the one making up the stories. And she did it all the time."

"Not all the time," Nellie interrupted.

"Well, most of the time. A lot of the time anyway. We alternated where we had our Literary Society meetings, and, when it was her turn, she usually had several new pieces out, and had a tale ready for each one."

"I thought it was kind of fun." Mindy laughed. "I always looked forward to it."

"You would." Larabeth was not giving up her annoyance at the topic.

"Well, it was different, anyway. Not like the usual just eat and talk." Mindy did not hide her resentment at the last remark. "Since we don't do as much reading anymore. Not like what we used to."

"What were the stories like?" Peabody was trying to ease the slight tension. He wasn't here to mediate. Certainly not between women, if he could help it.

Susan responded, apparently having noticed the same thing he did. "She'd hold up something, say a piece of glass with a flower design, and narrate us a story. 'This was designed for the thirteenth birthday party of Princess Bertha Mae of Denmark. She used it on all her stationary and even embroidered into her clothes. From that point on, it was considered a good luck symbol in Denmark.' Then she'd add a fable of a time when it was not used and bad luck came about. It was just silly stuff, harmless enough. We just knew it was going to happen whenever we were here."

"Where did they come from? These objects. In real life, I mean."

Nellie shrugged. "She always had a lot of those things. Her shelves were full of them."

"I asked her once," Mindy added. "She just said, 'Here and there'. I think it was antique shops and yard sales. That's where you see that stuff."

"Was any of it valuable?"

"Not that I know of." Larabeth looked to the others for confirmation. They all shook their heads. "What does it matter?"

Peabody paused, but realized he was here to get information, so he may have to also provide some.

"Some of the pieces appear to be missing. From the cabinet in the living room. We noticed that many did not seem to fit her personality or her apparent interests and wondered why she had them. You have all helped me get an idea of why she had them, but now I'm still wondering how she got them and why someone would take some from her. So the theft could have to do with how she got them in the first place."

"I think she liked them being different than something she would pick out for herself," Susan said. "She once said something about Harry bringing some boxes over for her. That he liked to bring her something when he came to visit."

"Her nephew, Harry Townsend?"

"Oh, yes." Mindy smiled. "He was always visiting and bringing her things like that. He is such a good boy."

"You don't know where he got them from?"

They all shook their heads. Susan added, "We have no idea which pieces he may have brought. If any."

"And you're not aware of anything valuable among her collection? Anything that had a real story behind it?"

Susan moved the cheesecake away before he could take another piece. "If there was anything worth some money, I don't think she knew it. That isn't why she collected them. And she wouldn't have spent a lot of money on something like that. Come to think of it, she wouldn't have spent a lot of money on probably anything. Having expensive or valuable things just didn't matter to her."

Peabody recognized that there was probably no more relevant information to be obtained, and no more cheesecake as long as Susan was watching what he ate.

"Thank you ladies for your time and for the wonderful dessert." He paused, giving somebody time to offer "One more for the road?" but Susan seemed to have made it pretty clear. "You have been very helpful, and this does tell us some things we didn't know before."

As he left, Peabody considered what he had really learned. The odd collection had been used to inspire and tell stories, but that didn't explain why some were now missing. And what the heck did it have to do with her death?

# CHAPTER 13

After Stephanie Reasoner entered the Summerfield Bank, she stopped and gazed around the high-ceilinged open lobby. It wasn't very busy yet at this time of day, and off to the right, she found Harry Townsend, Mel Johnson, and Charlene Matthews, the bank manager, talking in front of the door to the safety deposit vault. She walked in that direction as they looked up.

"Steph," Johnson said. "You know Charlene, don't you?"

"Ms. Matthews." Reasoner nodded at her. "I assume Mr. Townsend has informed you why we are here."

"Yes, Stephanie, he did. You want to see Grace Mathison's safety deposit box." Matthews held out a piece of paper. "I understand this is a murder investigation..."

"Let's say suspicious death at this point." Reasoner wanted to avoid overusing the word "murder" around Townsend.

"Oh," Matthews looked down at her paper. "I had them fill in 'murder' on this form. It's for you to sign saying you're taking responsibility for opening the box. I don't know if..."

"That's okay. We'll go with that for now." Reasoner took the form from her, walked over to a table to get a pen, and signed the form at the bottom. "Is that all we need?"

"Normally, no. But we all know Mrs. Mathison has died and that the police department has to have access to anything that may help solve her...suspicious death." Matthews took the form. "Harry, do you have the key?"

He nodded at Reasoner who handed over the small red envelope and then he signed the entry book. Matthews unlocked the outer vault door, checked the number of the right box, used two small keys to unlock that box's panel, and then left them to it.

Townsend asked, "Is it okay if Mel stays? He may recognize something that I don't."

Reasoner hesitated, but figured Johnson had been part of much of this already, so she merely shrugged.

Townsend pulled out the small box and set it on the table in the middle of the vault. He looked at Reasoner, lifted the lid, and pulled out an envelope.

"This says it's her mortgage. Should we check?"

Reasoner nodded. "I think we need to check everything just to make sure." She had her official Summerfield Police Department Log out so that she could note the contents. "And we want to do it with both of us here."

Townsend opened the envelope. It was the mortgage with Paid and the date stamped across the front. He put it next to the box and pulled out the next set of papers.

"Insurance. Here's home insurance, car insurance, and life insurance. Should I see the details on the life insurance?"

"You're going to have to know them at some point. Let me look at it." She took that paper from him. "It look likes the beneficiaries are you and your sister. The total is for one hundred thousand. So the two of you take out funeral costs and split what's left."

"I didn't know. Honestly, I didn't."

Reasoner looked at Johnson.

"I knew, but I never shared it with Harry. That was Grace's business."

"Okay, we'll determine if that's true later, but for now, I'll accept that." Internally she made a note to check into Townsend's finances to determine if he might have had an immediate need for that kind of money. "What else do we have?"

"Her will." Townsend handed it straight to her. "She never told me what was in it."

Reasoner glanced through it, just to make sure that it looked typical and that there weren't any surprises. "All right. This information you'll need to hear from her lawyer. But it looks fairly standard. Next."

Some miscellaneous papers were in a manila folder marked, appropriately, "Miscellaneous". It included a statement of her diamond ring's value, as of forty years ago, several receipts for various structural improvements around the house, a listing of the house contents and furniture, and a couple of older letters.

"From the looks of it, I don't think this list of the contents has been updated in over ten years. Probably not very reliable now," Reasoner noted. "And these letters," she took a brief look, "appear to be personal, oh...very personal letters from Ralph. And a picture. You may not want to see these, but apparently, she had reason to keep them." She put all of the papers in a pile.

"I would like, with your permission, to have Ms. Matthews make copies of all of these, except for the personal letters, just so that there's no question of what was originally in here, then put these back. That okay with you? I don't see anything significant offhand, anything that's relevant to her death, but we had to look."

Townsend looked down at the pile. "Yeah, okay, I guess that's okay."

"We'll take a more in-depth look later, but I don't expect to find anything. It looks pretty usual for what people would keep here."

Townsend breathed out as if he had been holding it in for a long time. "Well, I didn't think there would be anything. Aunt Grace wasn't the type of person to have any big secrets."

Reasoner left the vault, and the two men watched her hand the collection of papers to Charlene Matthews. Within a few minutes, they returned the papers to the box and returned the box to its place, and left the vault together. Townsend now seemed anxious to leave.

"I need to get back to the office. Is there anything else that we need to do, that you need us for? If not, I've been gone a long time, and there are things I probably need to do." Johnson nodded in agreement and looked at Reasoner as if for permission to leave.

Reasoner was surprised at the comment as neither one had any reservations about leaving earlier. "I imagine Sherri has everything under control. But for the moment, I think we are done here. Have a good afternoon, and thank you again for your assistance today."

Once they were outside, Townsend started to walk off, realized he was going in the wrong direction and had to turn around in front of Reasoner. He smiled embarrassedly. "Just distracted I guess. You have a good day." Johnson was waiting for him on the sidewalk.

Very distracted, Reasoner thought. Very distracted indeed.

# CHAPTER 14

Somewhat distracted himself, Jeff Pierson walked into Conference Room A to find another plate of fresh baked goods sitting in the middle of the table. Where does Hazy get these, he thought. We don't have a budget for them. Is she dating the baker?

The board was organized much more neatly than before – Hazy's handiwork again. Legible and easy to follow, certainly not his own typical method of communication.

The others followed, one at a time, with Peabody finding his seat and a doughnut just at the four o'clock appointed meeting time. No mayor or crime scene people this time. Hazlett stood next to the board with the chalk firmly in her hand. She was not going to let Pierson mess up her carefully crafted columns or neatly written notes.

He started to stand, realized Hazlett was already there and glaring at him, then moved around the corner of the table so he could face the board and sat back down.

"Okay, Hazy will now apparently be taking the notes for us. So where are we? Did anyone come up with anything new?"

Addams cleared his throat. "I took a specific look at the items reported stolen from garage sales. Many of the smaller ones are in Mrs. Mathison's curio shelves. Only a couple of the missing ones were on the list, though. The Laurel and Hardy statuette..."

Reasoner chimed in, "That's what Harry Townsend confirmed it was."

Addams nodded and continued, "And a small pottery bowl. The problem is that many of these types of items were to be sold in boxes of miscellaneous things, and the homeowners couldn't always remember just what had been put in those boxes. If anything was going to be sold individually out of those boxes, it was going to be for a dime or a quarter, maybe a dollar. Nothing considered worth stealing, or specifically reporting stolen."

"Unless it had some personal value to the person reporting it." Pierson opened his mouth again as if he wanted to say more, but decided not to and waved it off. "Just go on."

"Unless, as Jeff said, it was personally valuable to the person who reported the thefts. But then, if it was that personally valuable, why did they put it in a box of junk?"

"Why indeed?" Pierson interrupted again. Reasoner turned to look at him, but he ignored her.

"So some of her collection shows up on the lists, but not a lot. Which may explain where they came from originally, but not why she has them or how they came into her possession."

Peabody brushed some crumbs off his lip. "Well, I can give you some ideas as to why she has them, but not how she got them." He straightened up in his chair. "According to the illustrious members of the Summerfield Literary Society, these objects were her stories."

"What?" Reasoner asked.

"Her stories. Apparently, when she was teaching, she used to bring in a box or a bag of small objects and have her students pick a particular one out and write a story about that object. It was a prompt for creativity."

"All right," Reasoner said slowly. "But she's not teaching now."

"My wife says she still uses, excuse me, used them for made-up stories, only now she does, did the telling."

"Your wife?" Pierson was puzzled.

"My wife, Susan, is a member of this book club. It didn't occur to me right away this morning that it was the same club. I knew who the members were, but I never have anything to do with them, just to say 'hello' to. I had the least contact with Grace Mathison, and never put it together with Susan's book club. Anyway, Susan said when Grace hosted the club meetings, she usually pulled out some odd piece and made up a story about it. I don't know if she just wanted to be creative or was actually fantasizing that she owned something significant, but that's what she would do. So Susan says. Sometimes it was interesting, sometimes apparently not. That doesn't explain how she got them, but it may be why she had such a varied collection. Why things didn't particularly match each other."

From her position in front of the board, Hazlett asked, "Did anyone know if she went to these yard and garage sales?"

Peabody shrugged. "They assume she did, but no one really knew. They didn't go with her, if she did."

"So now we've got a 'where they came from' and a probable 'why she had them', but not a 'how they got to her'." Addams picked up his lists. "And none of the bigger items have turned up – the clocks, the speakers, the toaster ovens, the valuable jewelry, the first edition books, those types of things. None of them are reportedly worth all that much, not according to their owners, but they were worth something, probably in the twenty to fifty dollar price range at these sales, maybe a little more to a collector or an antique dealer."

"Bud, can I see those lists?" Reasoner held out her hand. He passed them over to her, and she quickly scanned through them.

"Okay, so we've got some information regarding her collection, but we don't know if it has anything to do with her death." Pierson sighed. "It could be that the missing objects were simply given away by her. Her friends don't seem to attach any significance to them. They certainly don't appear to be valuable. We don't know what it means."

"Except that she wasn't supposed to have them," Addams said.

"So that's a mystery. It may be hard to believe that she accidentally ended up with so many from our stolen property lists, but maybe she picked them all up from some disreputable junk dealer. But we're here to investigate her death, not junk worth a dollar." He turned to Reasoner. "Speed, do you have anything to tell us from your morning interviews? Any problems with Harry Townsend?"

Reasoner had stopped her scanning and was staring at a spot on one page.

"Speed?"

She slowly put the paper down, then looked at Pierson and nodded.

"Yes, Jeff. But not any problems with Mr. Townsend." She opened her log and took a minute looking at it. "I don't have anything really vital to report. Mr. Townsend and I went through the house together, as well as with Mel Johnson. The only thing of any significance was that he did notice that some shelves in the cabinet looked different as if some pieces were missing. But he didn't know what they were till I specifically told him. He acted very shocked when I told him where she had probably been killed. I wasn't sure at first that I wanted to tell him, but I did want to see what he would do. Unless he's a very, very good actor, I think his reaction was genuine.

"However we did find quite a bit of money hidden in tea boxes in her kitchen cabinet. Much more than one would have expected to be put away as rainy-day money through the week. For right now, we have no information as to where it came from. Phil Culbertson is looking at all the contents of her kitchen cabinets right now.

"At the bank, we went through her safety deposit box, but nothing in it except personal papers -- the will, insurance, home improvement receipts, things like that. I made copies of everything, and I'll take a closer look at them, but I didn't see anything relevant to her death or her collection."

"Offhand, anything stand out to you?" Addams asked. "Anything that might tie in at all for a possible motivation?"

She shook her head. "Just the money from her will and insurance, but it's not enough to make somebody rich from her death. I'm going to further check Townsend's finances, but it's hard to believe he would have killed his own aunt for that amount."

Pierson drummed his fingers on the table and looked up at the board. Hazlett had filled in where she could, but it didn't really add much to what they already knew. Which wasn't much to start with. There was a lot of miscellaneous information with no apparent connections.

"We still have a harmless little old lady, sorry, Pops, not that old, who was liked by most everybody and didn't have anything worth taking, much less killing for. A worthless collection of knick-knacks, with some missing that may, or may not, have been there at the time of her death." He looked back at the others. "We might be reaching on trying to tie those in with her death. No viable motive and no viable suspects. Not much to go on."

There was a quiet moment while everyone seemed to be considering what he had just said.

"Chief," Reasoner spoke up. "I've been thinking. What if..." She took a breath. "What if her death was an accident, not a murder, not intentional?

If the real issue was trying to cover up an accident, not a killing?"

Hazlett wrote "ACCIDENT?" under the MOTIVE column in big bold letters.

Addams spoke, "You mean, if, and I'm just throwing this out, putting her on the roof was to make it appear to be more of a natural accident, rather than one caused by someone?"

Reasoner continued. "There doesn't appear to be a plan here anywhere. It just looks as if...it happened, and the rest was improvised, taking advantage of the storm. We can't find any reason to kill her, or anybody that would have wanted her dead. The only ones that benefit at all would have been Harry Townsend and his sister, but, by all accounts, their relationship was good. There were no conflicts or money problems."

"He did seem very shook up by it," Pierson said.

"But an accident?" Peabody questioned. "She was hit in the head!"

"Kind of personal for someone that everybody liked," Reasoner agreed. "Can you picture somebody coming up on her and purposefully doing that? From Dr. Ross' description, the front left temple over the eye, it would have had to have been from the front. I don't see anybody planning on facing her and doing it on purpose. Do you?"

"Well, we haven't found anyone yet." Addams emphasized the "yet". "But you're right. No one can think of anyone that would do that."

Reasoner continued. "I'm just asking that we consider the possibility. Which moves motive in a completely different direction, to one where somebody was just momentarily upset or confused, not angry or vindictive. A minor conflict that went ... that went way beyond what was intended." She looked at Pierson. "That could then tie in with the missing pieces from her collection. The pieces that she wasn't supposed to have."

"Something to consider." Pierson looked again at the board. Hazlett had long ago put "Missing Curiosities" under motive, and now she underlined it. With a star in front. He took a moment, then brought his gaze back to the others.

"Does anybody have anything they want to add?"

"That does bring it back to including friends, people with nothing to gain," Addams said.

Pierson looked at his watch. "It has gotten past suppertime. Why don't we sleep on it tonight? We've got some information, but I think we need time to figure out where we are going with it." He reached toward Reasoner. "Speed, let me have those lists. Maybe I can spot something there since we now think they may be significant. Bud, I think you've got duty tonight, but, if something serious comes up, you let me know."

Pierson noted that Peabody picked out a bear claw and wrapped it in a napkin. He shook his head, knowing that Peabody's wife would have supper ready, but that Pops liked to be prepared if that dinner included a big salad.

Reasoner watched the others drift back to their desks. Pierson headed to his office, started to close his door, but left it open. He sat down behind his desk and set the list of stolen items in front of him.

Addams picked up the phone for emergency calls from Hazlett's desk, then sat down at his own, looking between a pile of what appeared to be old paperwork and a blank tablet. He pulled the tablet over and started writing on it. The duty officer for that night usually stayed a couple of hours in case somebody walked into the station with an emergency, then took the mobile phone home with him/her to answer nighttime calls. He was apparently settling in for a while.

Reasoner wandered around the office. She took a look at the night duty roster posted on the wall and noted that she had the following night. She went out back to the parking lot with their regular cars. Peabody was pulling out, but the others were still inside. There were two gray sedans. Well, we knew there were quite a few in town, she thought. She walked around to the back and took a look at the bumpers and the stickers in the windows. Everybody seems to have some sort of sticker, she thought. Her own car bore one for a local gym, *Fitness by Fleming*, because the owner was a good friend of hers.

She started to pull out the keys to her car, but looked at them for a few seconds and returned them to her pocket. She reentered the station and walked up to the open door for Pierson's office.

He looked up before she knocked. "Speed? Aren't you going home?"

"Jeff, could we...talk for a little bit?"

He set the papers carefully down and squared them off neatly. "Sure, Speed. Do you want to close the door and take a seat?"

"How about?" She looked out the front door at the green. "Could we go talk outside? On the green, at the bandstand? I've always liked that spot."

"Okay...if that's what you want." He rose and pulled on his jacket. "Gets a little chilly as the evening comes on. Going to put yours on?"

"Yeah, I should." She moved across the room to pull her jacket off the back of the chair at her desk and joined him at the front door.

Pierson called to Addams. "Bud, we're going to be back, so don't lock the front door till you see if we've returned."

Addams waved without looking up.

# CHAPTER 15

Reasoner paused just outside the door to take a look around the green. Shops were still open, but some of the businesses were closing their doors and people not already at home for supper with their families, were heading to Mac's Café or The Silver Griddle for their late evening meal. Not many other choices. Pierson stopped with her, but his eyes were on the ground.

The night was graying with the beginning of dusk, but the street lamps weren't on yet, and it was still light enough to appreciate the intimacy of the small town. A couple of people were cutting through the park covering the green, but there was no one at the bandstand, and she led the way there.

Two or three folding chairs were leaning against the wall inside for just-in-case-they-were-needed moments, but she didn't pull them out. The structure was six-sided, with one open to the steps and the others all half-walls and a single railing above each, posts at each corner holding up the overhanging roof. Reasoner stepped up into the bandstand and put her hands on the top railing of the half-wall farthest from the opening and facing the police department, and just stood there for a moment.

Pierson joined her. "I've always liked this time of night. Enough light and sounds to recognize where you are, but it's quieter and calmer. Easier to appreciate. I think it's difficult to get this in the big city."

"Yeah." Reasoner absently scratched at a spot on the railing. "Sometimes, I... wish there were more excitement. More things happening, more drama, more activities, just more. But then I realize I'd get tired of that quickly, maybe overwhelmed, and that I'd miss this. This whole town is a family, our family. And what happens to one of us here impacts all of us."

She took a deep breath and turned. "Jeff, what happened?"

"What?" He tried to look startled, but it was as if he'd been practicing the reaction. "What do you mean?"

"Jeff, you had duty that night." She put her hand out to touch his arm. "If Mrs. Mathison was going to call anyone that night, it would have been you."

"But. . . " he started to say something, then stopped and stared unseeing at the station.

"That was one of the big questions. Who would have been there at that time and in that weather? None of her friends or neighbors was going to be out. Harry Townsend was in another town. It was likely to be someone that she had a reason to call and ask to come over. And she has a history of calling us.

"Mrs. Bucholtz reported seeing a gray sedan with a circular sticker in the rear window. Both you and Marie have your bowling league stickers in your back windows. With the big round bowling ball logo. All you would see from across the street, in the rain, would be a big circle."

He took a step away from her, but continued to fix his eyes in the far distance. "There are plenty of those around town. As you said, even Hazy has one in her window." But there wasn't a denial in his statement, and he still didn't look back at her.

"But Marie's name isn't on any list of stolen objects from a garage sale. Yours and Judy's are. Specifically reporting the stolen statuette and the pottery bowl from your garage sale. The objects missing from Mrs. Mathison's house. Nothing from anybody else's list. The only things missing are from your house. And the bowling trophy makes sense too. It wasn't on the list of stolen property, but I'm betting it was yours.

"And someone had to have been strong enough to carry her body onto the roof, as well as know there was a reason for her to be out there. To rescue her cat, Reginald. Marie has the gray sedan and the bowling logo, but she's not strong enough to carry a body up there. You are. And not that many people know about the cat getting up on the roof. You do.

"So, Jeff." She took a step toward him. "What happened?"

Pierson finally turned his gaze from the station and took a few steps to the open side of the bandstand. He sat on the top step facing the mayor's law office. Reasoner sat beside him. He put his head in his hands and shuddered.

"Oh, my God. Oh, my God. What have I done?" He started rocking, and Reasoner put her arm around him. "What have I done?"

"I'm not going to say, 'it's alright', because it's not. But I am going to be here for you." She paused. "It was an accident, wasn't it?"

He took a deep breath and finally looked up. "Yes, you were right about that. It was an accident. I never meant to hurt her."

"I know, I know." She murmured, not sure if he even heard her.

"I just turned, and she was right there." He shook his head as if he still couldn't believe it.

"Just tell me what happened, Jeff. I believe you."

"She called. I had...I had stayed late because of the storm coming and was just getting ready to leave. I really didn't want to go over there, that stupid cat, but," he ruefully smiled, "I didn't want her going out on the roof. Which she would have if no one else had shown up."

He wrung his hands then spread his fingers. "I want to say it was raining cats and dogs, but it was just one cat. I set the ladder up out back and managed to get the cat down. I've done it often enough now that Reginald doesn't fight it like he used to. Grace offered me something to drink, something with a little bite to it. I don't want to drink on duty, but I was wet and cold, and it wasn't much, and I was going straight home."

The sky was now getting darker and a few streetlights at the corners were turning on, but they didn't notice.

"While she was drying Reginald, I wandered over to her cabinet in the living room. I'd never really looked at it before. I didn't think much of it, and she didn't think much of my going over there. I saw the Laurel and Hardy statue. I just thought it was curious at first, that she would have one too, I didn't imagine there were too many of those around. Then I saw the bowling trophy, and I leaned in closer." He looked at Reasoner, but not really seeing her. "It had my name on it! It was mine! I didn't even know it was gone. I thought it was still in a drawer upstairs. Judy must have put several of my things into a big box for the garage sale and not told me, figuring I wasn't going to miss them. Not really. She probably didn't list it as stolen because she still didn't want me to know it was gone. That and the train locomotive. One of my favorite toys as a kid.

"I must have yelled something when I saw it. I picked it up and turned around. She was right there! Right in my face!" He put his hands up. "She was looking angry and shouted, 'Leave those alone!' She was coming right at me, closer than I would have thought. I just put my hands out and didn't think about my holding the trophy and it hit her right in the side of her head. And she went down. Just like that." His hands came down. "Just like that."

"Why didn't you call an ambulance?"

"I knelt down, but she was gone. Her eyes were open and staring, and there was no pulse. I started toward the phone, but stopped just before I got there." He looked at Reasoner, seeing her for the first time. "Speed, Steph, I'm the police chief. I'm the one that's supposed to keep people from getting killed, not the one killing them. I know everyone would have believed it was an accident, but how can anybody trust a police chief that kills someone, even if by accident?"

He looked away again. "She was gone. There wasn't anything I could do for her. I knew that. That damn cat walked over to her then. That damn cat. I wanted to put him back on the roof and forget this ever happened." He sighed. "And that's what I decided to do. I took him back up there, then carried her body up. I tried to get her to roll off the roof so that she would land on the ground. I know, it sounds gruesome, but I thought that if she fell to the ground, any damage to her head would be assumed to be because of the fall. That people would think what they first thought, that she went out to get the cat on her own and slipped. But she got caught up on the edge of the vent, and I couldn't get to her in the storm, to finish it.

"I went back inside, cleaned up what I could of the carpet, washed the glasses, and took the knick-knacks that I knew were mine. Including the trophy. They're in a box in my garage. I couldn't remember what I had touched and what I hadn't."

"So that's why you went on the roof first. And why you kept touching things in the house." Reasoner remembered.

"Yeah, I didn't know what evidence I had left, if any. I picked up a screw on the roof. I don't know where it came from, but I took it just in case." He took it out of his pocket to show her, but she wouldn't take it, and he put it back in the pocket.

Reasoner stood up. "Jeff, I'm going to have to arrest you, you know that.

I believe you, but I'm going to have to take you into custody."

He looked up at her. "Can you give me a minute, Steph? Just to get myself together? As you said, this is a nice evening, and it's going to be the last time I get to enjoy it for quite awhile."

She looked at him for a moment, closed her eyes and then nodded. "Alright, I'm going to walk over to the station and tell Bud what's going on. But if you're not there in ten minutes, I'm going to have to come back and get you." She put her hand on his shoulder. "We'll get through this, Jeff."

"Okay, I'll be there. I promise."

She walked off into what had become darkness, disappearing behind the bandstand into the trees.

———   ———   ———

Pierson sat by himself, not thinking of anything in particular, but taking in the early night air, possibly for the last time in a while. It was dark by now, and there really wasn't anything to see, maybe a figure farther down the street or moving across the green. The quiet was calming, and his breathing was starting to return to normal.

He heard a scream.

# CHAPTER 16

Martin Addams jumped at the scream and ran to the outer door of the station. Outside, there were lights on the streets and from some of the businesses, but the green itself was dark. A few people on the sidewalks were moving tentatively in the direction of the park, but it took a few seconds for him to make out a figure running from the bandstand to what appeared to be someone lying on the ground behind it.

He sprinted in that direction. As he got closer, he saw it was Pierson kneeling next to the body, crying "No, no, no." Addams pulled his radio off his belt and keyed in for medical emergencies.

"This is Officer Martin Addams from Summerfield Police. We need an emergency medical vehicle to the south side of the village green in front of the police station. There is a person down apparently injured, but I do not know the extent of the injuries."

He received a response that a vehicle was on its way and he stepped closer to Pierson. Pierson was now sitting holding the head in his lap, and Addams could see it was Stephanie Reasoner. There was blood on the front of her uniform, and her eyes were only half open.

Pierson was slightly rocking. "It's all my fault. It's all my fault. Everything is my fault. Stay with me, Steph. It will be alright, just stay with me."

Addams knelt next to them, then looked up to see others standing about ten feet away. He recognized Hank Peters from the hardware store.

"Mr. Peters, there's an emergency squad on the way. Watch for it and bring it here."

Peters hurried to the edge of the street, ready to wave the ambulance down.

Addams reached out a hand to Pierson. "Jeff, what happened? What's going on?"

Pierson looked stunned. "I just told her what happened! It's all my fault! Don't you see?"

"Jeff, I don't know what you're talking about. What happened here?" He pointed to Reasoner's wound. "Did you see anything?" He reached over to the front of her uniform, hesitated for just a second, then unzipped her jacket, unbuttoned the shirt, and pulled it open to see where the blood was coming from. There was blood flowing from a long slit just below her chest. He pulled out a handkerchief from his back pocket and pressed it to the wound.

Reasoner's eyes slid over to him, and she whispered something. He leaned in closer and she said it again, slightly louder but with great effort, "Why did he do it, Bud, why did he do it?"

"Who, Steph, who?"

But her eyes closed and she coughed gently, turning her head into Pierson's chest.

Addams pressed the cloth harder and heard the ambulance arriving. Peters was yelling, "Here, over here!" and there was the sound of the doors opening and people hurrying. Then they were next to him pushing him aside and pulling Pierson away from Reasoner.

Jim McGarry was the EMT asking him, "Is there anything I should know, Bud?"

"Bleeding is in front. Appears to be more of a knife wound than a gunshot. Don't know if there's anything more. No idea how this happened."

"Got it. We'll take it from here." He lifted the cloth briefly to look, then pressed it back down and quickly examined her for any other signs of injury. He and the other EMT loaded her onto the stretcher, then into the back of the squad. "We'll take her to Memorial. They have the trauma unit." They took a few minutes to get medical care started then sped away, sirens once again breaking the night stillness.

Mayor Plummer moved out of the growing crowd. "Jeff, Bud, I just got here. Was that Stephanie? What happened?"

Pierson, now standing, was sobbing. "Will you just quit asking me 'what happened'? Everything happened!" He threw up his hands, and then they fell back by his side.

Addams and Plummer looked at each other and just stood there for a moment. Pierson took two deep, shuddering breaths, then one more and held up his left hand.

"Okay, okay. Bud, we're going to need to talk. JJ, you might as well be there, too. But I need to call a lawyer first, some other lawyer, JJ. "

They started walking back towards the station, away from the onlookers still in the park. Hank Peters ran up to them, "Is there anything else I can do?"

Addams turned to him, "No thanks, Mr. Peters. I appreciate your helping with the ambulance. We'll let people know what's going on with Stephanie. And we'll get back with you and the others to ask if anybody saw anything." He paused. "Did you see what happened?"

"No, no I didn't. And I doubt that anyone else did. We were all just closing up. But I'll let the others know that you'll get with us. Tomorrow morning?" Adams just waved his hand and Peters reluctantly walked back to the small group waiting to hear what he had to say.

Pierson waited till Peters was out of earshot, then quietly said, "I'm the one that killed Grace Mathison." That stopped both of the others. "Stephanie figured it out and told me out there, at the bandstand. She was coming back to the station to get you, Bud, and arrest me. It's my fault she got hurt. I didn't do it, and I don't know just how she got stabbed, or who did it, but I know it's my fault. I'll tell you what I did, but I don't want to say it over and over." He shook his head. "Let me do it one time when I have a lawyer present."

He started walking back to the department with his head down. Neither Addams nor Plummer said a word, but followed at the same slow pace.

They entered the station to find Hazlett standing just inside the front door.

"Word travels fast in this town," she started, but Pierson walked right past her, so she looked at Addams. "Was it Stephanie? Is she okay, I mean..."

"It was Steph. She was apparently stabbed. We don't know who or why yet. I think she was still alive when they took her in the ambulance. We don't know anything beyond that."

"Bud?" Pierson had stopped just outside his office. "Do you mind, is it okay if I use the phone in my, in the office? I need to call...who would you suggest, JJ?"

"Matt Laurenfeld would be good, I would think." Plummer shrugged. "It's been a long time since I had anything to do with a courtroom. But he's experienced and generally knows what he's doing." He turned to Addams. "I'm not used to recommending other attorneys." He gave a nervous laugh, but nobody joined in.

"Thanks, JJ. And my wife. Oh God, I have to tell Judy."

Addams waved at the door. "Yeah, Jeff, go ahead."

As the door closed behind him, Hazlett looked puzzled. "A lawyer? What does he need a lawyer for? He didn't have anything to do with Stephanie, did he?"

Addams shook his head. "No, he…" Just then, Peabody came in through the back door, and Addams waited for him to get closer. "Jeff just confessed to killing Grace Mathison." Both Hazlett and Peabody stepped backward and sat down hard on the edge of a nearby desk. "We don't know anything more than that. He's going to give us the details when he has a lawyer present. And George, Steph is on her way to the hospital. She was stabbed, we don't know why, but it is serious." He put out a hand. "But not by Jeff. He didn't do that."

"I heard something had happened, but, good God!" Peabody muttered. More to himself than to the room.

Both Addams and Plummer pulled chairs out and sat down. They all sat in silence for a few moments. Plummer spoke first.

"I don't know about the rest of you, but this has been a bit overwhelming to me. A police officer stabbed, and the police chief confessing to a… murder."

"Well," Addams said. "I know Jeff wasn't responsible for stabbing Steph. He was running to the body just as I was."

"Did you see anybody else?" Peabody asked.

"I saw several people out as I was running over to the green, but nobody that I could say was particularly running away, and I'm not even sure who else was there." Addams looked up as if he was trying to recreate the moment in his mind. "I know Hank Peters was there. I asked him to wait for the ambulance. And I think Charlene Matthews, the bank manager. Maybe Mel Johnson, his office is right there. Maybe." He shook his head.

"But right now, I can't recall anybody else, just that there were people. I was focusing on Jeff and who I later found out was Steph."

He leaned his head back to look at the ceiling. "Oh crap." He turned to Peabody. "George, we need somebody to secure the area. I'll take you out and show you where I found them. We better do that now."

They had just returned when a car roared up to the rear of the building, the back door banged open, and Judy Pierson ran toward them. They all stood, but she didn't see who she was looking for. "Where's Jeff?"

Hazlett pointed at his office door. "Go right in. he'll be waiting for you."

Judy rushed to the door, opened it, released a sob and closed it again behind her.

"What should we do now?" Peabody asked.

Addams replied, "I'm going to wait for Matt Laurenfeld to get here, then we're all going to go into the conference room and hear Jeff's story."

"That makes sense," Plummer nodded.

"Marie, why don't you call Memorial Hospital and see if we can find out anything?" Addams asked her.

She called while they sat silently again and spoke quietly into the phone. Then she hung up and slowly returned to the group.

"She's in critical condition and is now in surgery. It's too early to give a prognosis. Did anybody call her parents?" She took their stunned silence as a "no" and returned to the phone. "I'll call them."

While they waited for her, the front door opened and Matt Laurenfeld came in.

"Gentlemen...and lady," though she wasn't listening. "I have a client I need to see."

Addams barely heard him but nodded toward the closed office door. He had his own thoughts to keep him company.

# CHAPTER 17

It had been a long night for Martin Addams. Of course, all nights are long when you don't sleep, but this one seemed to have set a record.

Judy Pierson had left crying, and then everyone had gone into the conference room for the interview with Jeff. His lawyer, Laurenfeld, had at first wanted to talk with him alone, but Pierson had insisted that everybody be there. He said he wasn't going to go over it and over it, at least not tonight, and the whole department had earned the right to hear him. Laurenfeld eventually gave in, but reserved the right to stop him at any time. He didn't.

When Pierson was finished with his statement, Addams and Laurenfeld asked any questions that needed to be asked. There weren't very many, and no one else said a word.

Pierson and Laurenfeld then did meet privately for a short period of time. Plummer left for home, to get what sleep he could. Hazlett had recorded the confession and interview and began transcribing it. She knew she wasn't going anywhere for the rest of the night. Addams and Peabody got flashlights and went back to the green to look for a knife or any kind of evidence. They also took police tape and cordoned off more of the area, as big an area as they guessed the crime scene unit would need. They came back an hour later, empty-handed, and Peabody went to his home to get what rest he could. They were going to be busy in the morning. After Laurenfeld left, Addams escorted Pierson to one of the cells.

"Jeff..." Addams began.

"Bud, there isn't anything to say." Pierson sounded exhausted. "I got myself into this. Now I have to pay the piper." He sat down on the cot, but looked up. "Any news on Stephanie?"

"Marie called again. She's out of surgery, but nothing's changed in her condition. They still don't know how she's going to do."

"It's all my fault, Bud."

"You didn't do this, Jeff. I really believe that. I saw you running toward her, not away."

Pierson lay down. "It's my fault, it's still my fault."

Addams shut the cell door from the outside and pocketed the key. He walked back to the desk area. Hazlett had run off copies of the transcription of the confession and handed him one.

"You're the arresting officer, you need to sign it," she said, "You could go home. I'm staying here."

"No, I have duty tonight, remember? This is my night." He took the copy and sat down at his desk.

— — —

George Peabody arrived back at 7:00 A.M. on the dot. Addams had never seen him come in that early or even close to it. Usually no one paid much attention to Peabody's hours. He just came in sometime and left sometime, and, in between, got done whatever he needed to do.

Hazlett had kept coffee going through the hours, and, somehow, there was a fresh plate of doughnuts. Addams could have sworn she never left. But then again, she also looked like she had slept all night and had put on a fresh, clean uniform. Addams rubbed his unshaven chin as Peabody absently picked up a doughnut and pulled up a chair next to him. Though he had gone home, he still looked as if he hadn't gotten any sleep either.

Peabody took a bite. It was a simple glazed doughnut, which wasn't usually his preference, but he didn't seem to care. If there was food there, he was going to eat it. "Stephanie?"

"Still the same as of twenty minutes ago. Not yet conscious, guarded condition."

Peabody nodded. "Susan is on her way over there this morning. To sit with her parents." He brushed a crumb off his shirt. "What are we going to do now, Bud? Where do we go from here?"

"The Grace Mathison case is closed. I'm waiting for a call from Sharon Alvarez from the district attorney's office. She'll be coming over sometime today – I assume this morning as soon as possible." Addams picked up a paper from his desk and studied it. "I know Hank Peters and Charlene Matthews were there on the green last night. And JJ. I also have the impression Mel Johnson was there somewhere. We're going to need a list from them of everyone else who was around. And then we'll need to interview them about what they saw, see if we can find a witness of some kind."

He stretched his arms and yawned. "And now, we definitely have to find a motive. This one was no accident. This was done intentionally.

"I read through Jeff's statement several times. He's the only with an immediate motive, but I know he didn't do it. I saw him running towards Steph as I was getting there. And he has openly confessed to Grace's death, so that actually removes the motive."

He looked at Peabody take his last bite. He thought it was the same doughnut, but wasn't sure.

"You and I are going to be busy today. We have to interview the witnesses, go through the papers Steph brought in last night, and somebody has to go out to Jeff's house to get the bowling trophy and the other evidence he said is in his garage. I also want to go back out to the Mathison house. Steph was in the house yesterday, maybe something is there that she didn't think was important but means more than she thought. I talked to Phil Culbertson from Crime Scene, but their department is still dealing with the gang war in Oldstown, and he will have to get here when he can. You and I need to go back over to the green as soon as there's enough light and look around again. There were a lot of people hanging around last night, so outside of a knife, I don't know what's there to be found."

The door that was rarely used, the connecting door to city hall next to the chief's office, suddenly opened and JJ Plummer came through. As usual, he was in a three-piece suit and looked ready for the day. Unusually, he ignored the plate of pastries. He strode over to where Addams and Peabody sat, waving Hazlett to join them.

"Bud, George, Marie. I have called an emergency town council meeting for eight o'clock this morning. It shouldn't take very long, but I'd like the three of you to be available as soon as it's over."

They all nodded, and Addams said, "Okay, we don't have anywhere to go quite yet."

Hazlett added, "I'm going over to the hospital soon after that then. Now that George is here, I think we're good with coverage in the station."

"I'll let you know when we're ready." Plummer turned and went back to his mayor's office.

"If you don't mind, after that meeting, and quickly before we figure out what else we have to do, how about if I go over to Jeff's house to get the evidence. I think it would be good for us to get that case wrapped up as soon as possible. Lord knows, I don't want to talk to Judy, but I've known her longer than you, and it may be easier for her to face me." Peabody had picked up another pastry. No point in them going to waste. As long as Susan wasn't around to glare at him.

Addams nodded. "I think that makes sense, George. You're also not the one that arrested her husband. When you get back, we'll sort out who does what from that point. Maybe I'll look at the papers Steph has on her desk while you're gone."

The three of them sat in silence, alone with their thoughts for the moment. They knew they would not be resting again until this attack was solved.

# CHAPTER 18

While they were waiting for the council meeting to end, Addams and Peabody had gone back to the green looking for the weapon used on Reasoner, expanding the range of their search to cover the entire area now that there was some light, but still had no luck in finding anything.

It wasn't quite 8:30 when Plummer returned and asked for the three of them to follow him back over to the town council meeting room. Around the table sat the current members of the council – Myron Stump, furniture-maker and current president of the council, Gladys Schumacher, the government teacher from Summerfield High School, and Cecil Skinner, the butcher from the Corner Grocery Store. Three chairs against the wall were also occupied. Mike Wannamaker was in one. The other two young men were strangers to the police officers, but apparently not to each other. They were identical twins.

Plummer waved the police officers to the more comfortable seats at the table, but he continued to stand.

"I have apprised the other members of the council as to what occurred last night. The events mean that, not only do we have a new crime to solve, but we are also down two police officers. You have our total support, but we do feel we have to address the loss of a police chief and the need for more manpower. You all know Mike, and he has had experience as police chief, but he believes, and we concur, that we need someone currently from the department and actively involved in the cases to be named at least interim chief at this time. We're doing this as an emergency measure, but with the expectation that it may become permanent once we have the time to address it properly.

"Bud, we'd like you to take the position at this time."

Addams started. "But, – but I'm the most junior member of the department. Surely George is better qualified."

Plummer looked at Peabody, but he strongly shook his head and said, "No way. No way at all. I'm way beyond any decision-making years."

"No offense, George, but that's along the lines of what we figured. Marie is employed by the police department, but is not an officer. Steph is, well, she's not here."

"Bud," Skinner spoke up. "It's not just that you're our only choice. We do honestly believe that you will do a good job."

"Well, maybe an okay job." Gladys Schumacher was known for her pessimism regarding change in any form. "I wanted to push Mike to come back or to get someone from Oldstown, but I was outvoted."

"Gladys." Plummer cocked an eye at her.

"Okay, okay. It was unanimous that we ask you." She still didn't sound like she was in agreement.

"What do you say, Bud? We've got other things to talk about, too." Stump gestured for Addams to respond.

"Alright." Addams spread his hands. "I'll do it. For now. When we get through this immediate crisis, I think we need to revisit this decision."

"Oh, we will," Schumacher agreed.

Plummer nodded, that agenda item having been taken care of. "The second point is that of manpower. We can't operate a police department, nonetheless an investigation of this magnitude, with a police chief, one officer, and a civilian office worker. Mike has agreed to temporarily help out in the office – taking phone calls, handling some paperwork, responding to any minor police needs outside the realm of this investigation, you know, such as a traffic issue or a juvenile complaint. I know Marie intends to go to the hospital following this meeting so Mike can be in charge of general office responsibilities when she is out."

Hazlett gave Wannamaker a thumbs-up sign. She had worked with him when he had been chief and trusted that he knew what he was doing.

"However, there is still the question of fieldwork. I wish we had someone that is both experienced and familiar with the people in this town. Unfortunately, we don't immediately have that option.

"We do have two young officers who graduated from the academy six months ago and have been filling in for vacations and sick leaves for the department in Oldstown. We actually have been trying to find budget money to hire one of them to fill that empty desk in your office, but now there is a need for both."

He waved a hand in their direction, and the two men stood. Addams could not see any difference between them, both in khaki pants and black long-sleeved shirts. This was going to be interesting.

"Sam and Seth Getty." Plummer wanted to point to them in turn, but hesitated when he realized he didn't know which was which. "They are from Plainfield, Ohio, so they grew up in a town similar in size to ours. As I said they have been working in Oldstown, and we have references indicating they have been providing satisfactory performances."

Both men turned to look at Plummer in response to the "satisfactory" comment, but he ignored them.

"The town council has just approved their hiring. Normally, the police chief would have been involved in the process, but, until three minutes ago, we didn't have one. As of now, they are on the clock, and ready to go.

"We did request assistance from the Oldstown Police Department as this is, at the very least, an attempted homicide. They are able to free someone tomorrow morning, a Detective," here he looked at a card in front of him, "Detective Joseph Krupke."

Plummer faced Addams. "Any questions?"

Addams grimaced. There were quite a few questions actually, but none that the mayor or town council would be able to answer.

"No, sir. Thank you for placing your trust in me. And for the added assistance. If you will excuse us, we do have a lot of work to do and the sooner we get to it, the better." He stood up. Peabody and Hazlett joined him. "Mike, Officers...Getty, it's time for us to adjourn back to our department."

He had just made his first decision as Acting Police Chief of Summerfield, but the others followed him as if he had been in charge for a while.

# CHAPTER 19

Once back in the department, Addams pointed to the available desks.

"Sam, you take that empty one. Seth, um, I guess you better take mine for right now, that one. We'll figure it out better when we have more time. Marie, before you leave, could you and Mike work on the badges and weapons and whatever else is immediately needed?"

Hazlett nodded then she and Wannamaker headed to the storage room and weapons lockers.

"Now." He looked at the two men. "How am I going to tell you apart? I don't need any confusion here."

One of them held up his right arm. "I'm left-handed, so I wear my watch on my right wrist."

"And I'm right-handed, so my watch is on my left wrist." The other one showed his left arm.

"Okay, but which one are you?" Addams pointed to the left-handed one. "I'm Sam."

"Sam, left. Seth, right. Sam, left. Seth, right. This may take a while."

Peabody pulled open a couple of drawers in Hazlett's desk until he found two visitor name tags.

"Here, put your names on these and stick 'em on your chests until Bud, I mean, Chief, here, gets your names down and we get you formal nameplates. Personally, I don't think you look all that alike."

"George, you should head out to the Piersons' to get that evidence." Addams continued his directions. "Take Seth with you as he might as well get started, then go and get lists of possible witnesses from Hank Peters, Charlene Matthews, and Mel Johnson. Oh, and JJ. Maybe he saw somebody I didn't. Sam, I want you to go out to the green as soon as we get you ready and see if you can find any trace of a weapon. George and I haven't found one, but maybe you have sharper younger eyes in the bright daylight. Then you and Mike start looking through these papers Officer Reasoner brought back to the office with her. I don't think there will be anything in them, but something prompted this attack. Until we rule it out, I think we're going to start with the assumption that this has something to do with her investigation into the death of Grace Mathison."

Addams moved the pile of papers from Reasoner's desk to the empty one assigned to Sam Getty. "I don't know what you're looking for, but anything that strikes you as – untypical. Let's go with that. I'm going back over to the Mathison house. Maybe Steph saw something there that the rest of us didn't. And somehow let that slip in the wrong place. We're just shuffling here right now, dancing one step at a time, but we start where we can."

Hazlett brought back a box and had the Gettys start signing cards for what equipment they were assigned. Wannamaker pulled up a chair next to Sam Getty's desk and started sorting the papers. Peabody picked through the doughnuts, seemingly looking for a crème-filled one now that he was paying attention. Addams looked at the door to the chief's office for a moment, but turned and walked out the back to a squad car. It was time to stop sitting and start doing something. Anything.

He drove slowly through the town. This morning it looked different to him. The sun was shining, dogs were barking somewhere, traffic was still moving. But he realized that the people on the sidewalk, instead of ignoring the squad car, were stopping and peering at it, trying to see who was driving. Who was left in the department to drive the car, who was still standing to do police business? Word may have traveled quickly, but details would have been sketchy. Now the word would pass that at least Bud Addams was still working.

He pulled up in front of the Mathison house behind a battered blue pickup truck with the ramp down. As he got out of the car, he heard a lawnmower from the back yard and walked around the house to find an older man with a baseball cap, smoking a cigarette at the far end of the property while pushing an antique, or at least really dirty and battered mower. The man hadn't noticed him yet, so Addams backed up to look at the roof and waited for the mower to finish circling the yard to reach him.

He noticed that the ladder was gone.

The mower neared and stopped, and Addams turned toward it. The man flicked ash from his cigarette behind a nearby bush and took a step towards Addams.

"Ayep, what can I do for you?"

Addams held out his hand.

"I'm Officer Martin Addams, sir. You are?"

"Emmett Doolittle." He took off his work glove, and they shook hands. "I do, did the yard work for Mrs. Mathison. Probably not going to get paid for this now, but it needed to be done today."

"Did you put the ladder away?"

Doolittle nodded, so slightly it was hard to tell, but he added, "Ayep. If left up, it's likely to fall over at some point."

"Yeah, that's probably okay by now. I could probably even be taking the police tape down. But I wanted one last look around." He pointed at the bushes and flowerbed. "You take care of all of this?"

"Ayep. Mrs. Mathison did some with the flowers out front, but she didn't really care about the back. If she sat out, it was on the front porch. I think she thought it was too damn quiet back here."

"I can see that. Did you enjoy working for her?"

Doolittle flicked another ash behind the same bush. "It was a job. It's what I do. She paid me, and she left me alone, so, yeah, it was good. The only thing she was particular about back here was to not touch that tall bush at the corner." He pointed to one that was about ten feet wide, very thick, and growing up past the roof.

"At the corner?" To Addams' eyes, it looked about a third of the way down the house.

"Ayep, there's a corner there. But the bush covers it so you can't hardly tell. Looks like the outside wall is just flush the whole way. But it's not."

Addams moved closer and leaned against the wall. The brick did come out several feet for the last part of the house, but he couldn't tell until he was looking closely. The size of the bush, almost a tree, interfered with the perspective.

"It's about two feet farther out there. I don't know why she wanted to hide it," Doolittle said.

Addams backed up into the yard so he could see the whole back of the house.

"That's the – the spare bedroom, isn't it?"

Doolittle shrugged. "I wouldn't know. I've never been inside. Well, not past the kitchen. She sometimes gave me something cool to drink."

Addams considered the corner for a minute. "I do believe I may be leaving that police tape up for awhile. I just may need to do that."

He turned to Doolittle. "Thank you, Mr. Doolittle."

"Just call me Emmett."

"Emmett. I do appreciate your assistance. That corner is something I didn't know."

Doolittle shrugged. "I don't think she wanted anyone to know. But it's been like that since I started working for her, since her husband died. That bush just kept getting bushier. Sort of stands out since I do trim back the rest, but she didn't want it touched. Not at all."

"Emmett, you do a good job. I'll make sure you get paid for mowing this time. But I can't speak for from now on."

They shook hands again, Doolittle put his glove back on, took a last drag from the little that was left of his cigarette, stubbed it out in the palm of his glove, and chucked it behind the same bush. Apparently that bush had grown on ash. He walked slowly back to the mower and started it up.

Addams took a last look at the corner, then took out a key as he moved to the back door, and opened it.

He quickly moved through the kitchen and living room to the hall closet. He thought he remembered a small tool chest in the closet, found it and took it down. Opening it, he poked through it for a moment till he found a tape measure.

He carried it to the first room on the left, the hobby room, found a clear path on the floor, and carefully measured the distance from the back wall to the front wall. Moving to the next room down, the spare bedroom, he repeated the process.

A full foot shorter. He took it again right next to the bed. The same distance, a foot shorter than the other room. But apparently, two feet longer on the outside.

There was an extra three feet somewhere.

He set the tape on the bed and moved over to the bookcase. He gave it a push. It was solid. He gave it a pull. It wasn't moving anywhere. He looked at the rest of the wall, but there wasn't anything else to move.

He sighed. He was going to have to move all the knickknacks off the shelves, but needed a place to put them.

He pulled his radio off his belt. "Mike, this is Bud. Anybody there?" With a small department, official calls weren't formal or often.

It took a few seconds for Mike Wannamaker to come on at his end of the call. "Hey Chief, this is Mike. What can I do for you?"

It took a second for the "Chief" to register. "Mike, I want you to send Sam out to the Mathison house. I could use a witness for something. Don't know what it means yet."

"Yeah, I can get him there. Look, we may have found something in this paperwork regarding that house. May have nothing to do with Steph's attack, but its information she had that we didn't. Only she may not have known she had it."

"What do you mean?"

"I'll send it with Sam. It may make more sense there anyway than my trying to tell you over the phone. Over and out."

"Um, Roger." The line went dead.

Addams was sure he recalled some empty boxes in the basement, and he went to find some. Returning with four medium-sized ones, he started filling them with the curios from the bookcase. The second shelf down he discovered a latch on the right side of the back wall. He flipped it, but still couldn't move the case, so he kept emptying the shelves. About halfway through the rest of the unloading, the front doorbell rang.

Opening the door, he found both Sam Getty and Emmett Doolittle on the front porch, with Doolittle glaring at Getty.

Getty started. "Chief, this man confronted me in the front yard and said he was keeping an eye on the place."

"Ayep, I did. I knew who you were, Officer Addams, but I don't know who he is. You got a regular police badge with your name, and I've seen you around town, but I ain't seen him before. And he's got one of them convention nametags, sort of fake, if you ask me."

"Emmett, he's okay. This is Officer Getty. We just hired him this morning. Brand new. Sam, this is Emmett Doolittle. He does the yard work here. He and I had a little talk this morning. Emmett, thank you for being cautious, but you can go back to work now. I got this."

Doolittle didn't look like he was too sure, but he slowly moved off back to the mower sitting idle in the middle of the yard.

"Come on in, Sam."

Getty followed him through to the back room. "Did you find anything on the green?" Addams asked over his shoulder.

"No, I didn't. Nothing that was immediately obvious anyway. No weapon." He held out a manila envelope. "Chief Addams, former chief Wannamaker wanted me to give you this."

"I'll look at it after we get this done." Addams set the envelope on the bed. "We need to get all these things off the shelves. Here's a box, just don't break anything."

Within a few minutes, they were done. There was a second latch two shelves up from the bottom. Addams flipped that one then stood up.

"Alright, Sam, we're going to see if there's anything behind this."

He grabbed the right side and was surprised to find out that now the whole bookcase moved easily, swinging open to the left. As the gap widened, a light came on behind it, apparently triggered automatically by the release of the door.

The light showed a three-foot deep closet the length of the room. Like the rest of the house, it was filled with miscellaneous objects. But, unlike the rest of the house, these appeared to have some value. Television sets, stereo speakers, some artwork, a couple of blenders, maybe a microwave. Toward the far right and left there were shelves with some books and small boxes on them. Addams whistled. These all appeared to be the larger items that were missing from the garage and yard sales.

"Sam, we may have solved ourselves another mystery." He stepped out. "Don't touch anything."

Addams keyed his radio again. "Mike, come in. This is Bud."

A few seconds later. "Yeah, Chief. Did you get those papers?"

"I haven't had a chance to look at them yet." He picked them up from the bed. "We have discovered a hidden room at the Mathison house. And it is full of what looks like stolen goods. I'm going to send Sam back to get the lists of property stolen from homes holding garage and yard and tag sales within the last six months. They may be on the desk in the chief's office. We were looking at them yesterday. You call Phil Culbertson from the county crime scene unit and have him meet Sam back here. Phil's probably over on the green, but he can leave one of his associates to that part of the investigation. I want him to see what he can find here, and I want Sam to check this inventory with those lists."

"Got it, but look at those papers I sent. I think that ties in with what you got there. Over and out."

"Uh, yeah." Wannamaker was gone before he could sign off himself. Addams opened the folder. It was a list of property improvements for the Mathison's home, going back several years. Wannamaker had starred the top page. It was the bill for adding a closet to the back of the spare bedroom, which had involved extending the room two feet into the back yard. The listed dimensions appeared to fit this hidden room.

Addams grinned at Getty. "We seem to have reached the same conclusion at the same time. You heard what I told Mike?"

Getty nodded.

"Then get to it. Mike will have that list for you. I'm going to wait till you get back, then I have some people to talk to. District Attorney Alvarez will probably be one of them. You will wait for Phil Culbertson from the crime scene unit -- you may have to vouch for him with Emmett out there. Don't touch anything till he gets here, then go through it with him, doing whatever he tells you to do. And check this stuff against the list of stolen goods. Got it?"

Getty nodded again and left.

Addams rubbed his chin, looking at the contents of the secret room. "Now we just have to figure out who's responsible for this and what this has to do with Steph's attack."

# CHAPTER 20

George Peabody drove out to the Pierson home with Seth Getty sitting beside him, looking very earnest, the way rookie cops look on their first day, trying to appear professional and experienced, but settling for not seeming overwhelmed.

"Take a breath. We got a long day ahead of us. No point in using up all your seriousness in the car. Save it for the witnesses."

Getty started to smile, but stopped as if he wasn't quite sure that was called for either. He did take a breath.

"So, Seth, you and Sam are brothers?"

Getty turned to directly face Peabody. "Yes, twins."

"Really? Fraternal?"

"No, identical. Most people can't tell us apart." He started to hold up his left arm. "I'm the right-handed..."

"Yeah, yeah, I saw that trick. But I don't think you look all that alike," Peabody shrugged. "Maybe when you dress exactly the same. I don't know."

Since Seth and Sam had both worn a long-sleeved black shirt and khaki pants that morning in lieu of a Summerfield Police Department uniform, Seth wasn't sure what to make of the remark.

"Well. Maybe when you're in uniform, huh?"

As they got out of the car, Peabody spoke again. "Remember, we're not here arresting anyone. We're just here to pick up what Jeff told us was here."

Judy opened the front door and drew a deep breath to compose herself, but still took a few seconds to open the screen door for them and gesture for them to come into the hallway.

"Judy."

"George."

"Judy, this is Officer Seth Getty. The town council just hired him this morning."

"To replace Jeff? Already?"

"To fill out the department. Nobody is replacing anybody. And we weren't consulted. They just presented him and his brother this morning as new hires. He is with me because, after this, we're going to talk to some people about Steph."

Judy put her hand to her mouth. "How is she? Any news?"

Peabody shook his head. "No. Nothing has changed."

"I am so sorry about what happened. You know Jeff would never have done anything to hurt her. She, all of you, meant the world to him."

"We know that, Judy," Peabody agreed. "We know he had nothing to do with the attack. That's not in question."

Peabody noticed Getty standing quietly, appearing to be trying to look more sympathetic than earnest, but not quite accomplishing either look.

Judy inhaled deeply again. "I suppose you're here for the box. It's still out in the garage. I was going to take it down, but Jeff said not to touch it. And, to be honest, I want nothing to do with it."

"That's okay, Judy, we'll handle it."

As they followed her through the kitchen, Peabody asked Getty, "Did Marie give you some gloves?"

"Yes sir." Getty pulled them out.

"Go ahead and put them on. I'll let you handle the box."

Judy pointed to a box labeled *Poindexter's Sporting Goods* on the top shelf. Getty reached up and pulled it down to his chest. It didn't appear to be heavy, but several objects shifted. He pulled back a flap and Peabody glanced inside.

"Yep, that appears to be what we're looking for." He looked at Judy. "Thank you. I know this has to be very difficult for you. I just want you to know that – that we're still here for you."

Impulsively he stepped forward and put his arms around her. She stiffened for a moment, then collapsed into his shoulder and started crying. "Oh, George. Oh, George, I don't know what I'm going to do." She was quiet for a few seconds. "I know I need to be strong for Jeff and for Jo. But…I never saw anything like this coming."

"Would you like Susan to come over? She can spend some time with you."

"I don't – I don't know. I don't know if I can face anybody right now." She pulled out a tissue and dabbed her eyes, then reflected for a few seconds. "But Susan has always been a good friend. If she doesn't mind."

"She won't mind. I'll call her. Can I use your phone?"

"Sure." Judy backed away and wiped the tears from her face. Peabody handed her a tissue to help. They went back into the kitchen, and he dialed the phone, remembering at the last moment to call her at the hospital.

Getty shifted the box slightly, as if not sure what he was supposed to do. Peabody shrugged at him, knowing that consoling the perpetrator's wife would not have been covered in training.

Peabody held out the phone to Judy. "Since Marie's now at the hospital, Susan thinks it's okay to leave Steph's parents. Here, she'd like to talk with you. We're going to see ourselves out."

To the sounds of audible sobbing from both ends of the call, the two men walked back through the living room and out the front door.

Once they were next to the car, they both took several deep breaths.

"Whoa," Peabody said. "I don't want to do that too often."

They got back in the car and drove back to the department. As they parked, Peabody pointed to the station. "Take that box inside and give it to Mike. Then come back out. We're going to walk next door to the hardware store."

— — —

Getty returned to find Peabody on the front sidewalk, looking at the window displays and the seasonal specials for Peters' Hardware Store. They entered together and approached Hank Peters rearranging a display of wrenches next to the paints.

Peters hung the last one, and they shook hands. "If I always leave everything exactly the same way, then customers don't need to ask me where things are. And in this business half of my service comes because of them asking me – the interaction between us, talking about their projects or what's going on in their lives. Most of them have learned just to ask me in the first place."

"Hank, this is Officer Seth Getty. Just started this morning. We'd like to talk with you for just a few minutes regarding last night."

"Sure, I was expecting you, or somebody anyway. How is Steph, by the way? Is she okay?"

"She's alive, but still in critical condition, Hank. Still touch-and-go."

"Ah, that's such a shame. I'll keep her in my prayers. Hey, Tommy, "he called to another man ringing up a sale at the far end of the counter. "Tommy, I'm going to the backroom for a minute. You got it?"

Tommy raised a hand without looking up and continued counting out change.

"Let's head to the back room, to my office. I spend as little time as possible back here, but I've got to have an office."

Within the small area, there was a desk with a swiveled rolling chair behind it and two hardback chairs in front, both piled high with papers and catalogues. The floor and all other surfaces were covered with miscellaneous boxes, tools, nails, and pieces of wire.

"Sorry about the mess. If I put something away, I never think about it. So I leave stuff out, so I know what I have to do yet." He looked around. "I guess what I really have to do next though, is clean some of this up. Hah." He picked up the piles from the chairs and set them on a corner of his desk. They started to lean, but he pushed them back and steadied them, brought his hands up and waited till he was sure they weren't going anywhere. He went around to his seat and waved a hand at the two chairs in front. The officers sat.

"So, what can I do for you? I didn't see the attack, if that's what you want to know."

Peabody first turned to Getty. "Did Marie give you a Summerfield Police Department notebook?"

Getty held it up to show he had it ready. "And a pen."

"Good. Turn to page one. You get to take any notes."

"Notes, huh?" Peters said. "So this is real official."

"Yeah, Hank. This is official." Peabody coughed slightly.

"Want a root beer drop?" Peters picked up a tin from under a paper and held it out.

"Thank you, I believe I will." Peabody took one. Peters offered the tin to

Getty, but he shook his head.

"Hank, we know you were on the green last night…"

"I was just locking up. Tommy…" He turned to Getty. "That's Tommy Delisle, my assistant out there. Tommy had already left a half-hour before. He was gone before any of this happened."

Peabody resumed his question. "As I was saying, you were there. I know you waited for the emergency squad. But who else do you remember being there at that time? Bud thinks that there were you and Charlene Matthews from the bank and Mel Johnson, but he was busy with Steph and couldn't picture anybody else specifically."

"Okay, there was Charlene. She and I usually leave about the same time. And, now that you mention it, I did see Mel come up from across the green, but I didn't talk with him. I think one of Charlene's tellers, but I couldn't tell you which one. And Harry Townsend, yes, I'm pretty sure Harry Townsend was there. But I think he showed up after the ambulance came. I pretty much talked with Charlene and that was it. There were a few more that arrived afterward. Like JJ Plummer, and Mrs. McMahon, walking her dog, and, I think, the girl Tracy Skinner, waiting for her dad from the grocery."

He shook his head. "That's all I can picture. If I think of someone else, I'll let you know."

"Thanks, that's helpful." Peabody watched as Getty scribbled down all the names. "That's m-a-h-o-n, not m-a-n-n." He turned back to Peters. "Now, what exactly did you see? Or hear?"

"Well, I heard the scream. Well, not really a scream, more of a cry out, you know what I mean? A cry of surprise, sort of. I had just taken a few steps toward the bank, cause I saw Charlene come out, when I heard it. But all I could really tell was that it had come from the green somewhere. By the time I realized it was in the direction of the bandstand, I saw Jeff Pierson and Bud Addams running toward a shape on the ground. I never saw anyone else near there. I heard Bud talking into his radio, then he saw me and told me to wait for the ambulance. So I went to the corner to wave it down.

"Then the other people started showing up, asking what was going on. By then we knew it was Stephanie." He shrugged. "That's all I got."

Getty spoke for the first time. "Did you pick up anything in the area? Anything that normally wouldn't be there?"

"No, I didn't pick up anything at all. I didn't see anything to pick up."

"Did you see anyone else pick up anything or throw anything away?"

"Nope. Can't say that I did."

Peabody asked one more question. "Did you see where Harry Townsend came from?"

Peters paused briefly, but shook his head. "No, sorry. I just know he was there once the ambulance came, but no idea where he was before. I would guess his office."

Peabody stood up, and Getty followed.

"Well, thank you, Hank. I appreciate your time."

"Sorry I couldn't help more." Peters rose to shake their hands. "As I said, I didn't see anybody over there before, and only Jeff and Bud right afterward. I hope to hell you catch whoever did this. Shoot, right out there on the green in the middle of town." He shook his head.

As they walked to the Johnson and Johnson Insurance Company next door, Peabody waved at the buildings surrounding the green. "Seth, this is the heart of Summerfield." He pointed specifically to a spot near the bandstand. "That's where Steph was attacked." Shaking his head, he continued, "I don't get it. I just don't get it. This is such a good place to live."

Peabody opened the door to the insurance office and waved Getty in ahead of him. Sherri Northrup was on the phone, and held up a hand when she saw who entered.

"Have to talk to you later, Lisha, the police have just come in. As well as somebody new that I definitely don't know yet. I'll let you know what's up when I hear something."

She hung up the phone and spoke to Peabody, but smiled in the direction of Getty.

"Hey, George, how's Steph doing?"

"Not too good. Last I heard, she was still in guarded condition."

Sherri's smile faded. "I'm sorry to hear that. She and I always got along so well. We'd talk and talk. Almost like we were best friends. What is this town coming to? First Mrs. Mathison, then Steph. Is someone after women, do you think? Should I be worried?"

The idea hadn't occurred to Peabody. "No, I don't think so, Sherri. I think it's something else going on."

"Well, good, because I'd hate to think we had one of those serial killers here in Summerfield. I mean, we don't even lock our doors half the time. Do you lock your doors?" The last comment was addressed to Seth Getty.

"Uh, yes, ma'am."

"Ma'am? I don't think I've ever been called 'ma'am' before. My name is Sherri, with an 'i', Sherri Northrup."

"Pleased to meet you. I'm Officer Seth Getty."

"New to the department, Sherri. Just this morning," Peabody interrupted. "Is Mel in?"

"Yes." She pointed. "Back in his office, that way."

"Thanks, we can find it."

Peabody and Getty passed the first room, where Harry Townsend glanced up from a stack of papers. Frowning, he stood up and followed them to the next office, where Mel was sitting. In the middle of the desk in front of him sat a small Newton's Cradle, the continuous pendulum where a swinging ball set in motion on one side of a series of balls transfers energy to a ball on the other side of the series. As they entered the room, the ends were slowing down, and Mel pulled one ball up to start it again.

Startled, he looked up and saw them standing in the doorway. "I'm sorry. It's been a traumatic few days." He waved at the Cradle. "This sometimes helps to calm my mind. Sometimes." He ruefully smiled and belatedly stood up.

"What can I do for you gentlemen? George, I don't believe I've met your friend." He put out his hand and Getty shook it.

"This is Seth Getty, a new officer just starting this morning. Mel Johnson. Harry Townsend."

Townsend, holding a pen in his right hand and continually clicking it, didn't offer his hand and didn't say anything. He simply stood, staring at the two police officers.

Johnson spoke, "A new officer, huh? It didn't take long to replace Steph." He breathed out and sat back down. "I'm sorry, there isn't any good way to say that. That was insensitive of me. I'm just babbling this morning."

That broke Townsend's silence. "We, we really are sorry to hear about what happened to her." But he didn't stop clicking.

"How is she by the way? Any better?" Johnson continued.

Peabody shook his head. "Still in serious condition."

"Has she said anything?" Townsend asked.

"No, she's been unconscious since she was taken in the ambulance." He turned to Johnson. "We understand you both were there last night." Johnson slowly nodded. "We'd like to ask you a few questions regarding who else was there and if you saw anything."

"Certainly. Please be seated. Harry...do you want Harry here?"

Peabody paused, then said, "It's up to you. We're just gathering information at the moment, see what anybody noticed last night. I have heard you were both there. It may save time to talk with both of you at the same time."

Johnson nodded and said, "I'm okay with that. Harry, could you bring in another chair from your office? Thanks."

Townsend brought one in, and Getty closed the door behind him. He pulled out his notebook as he took his seat and turned to a new page.

Peabody asked, "Could you tell me who you saw there at the green at the time of the incident?"

"Well, I didn't see the, uh, incident. I think I came up just after it. And I wasn't paying much attention to who else was around. I do believe Hank Peters was there, I think I remember Bud Addams asking him to wait for the squad. And Charlene Matthews from the bank." Johnson smiled briefly. "You usually see them together in the evening when their businesses close. No other time, but always then. I think there's a mutual interest there, but they don't want anyone to know, and they think they're getting away with it.

"Let's see. Also a young woman with Charlene, but I'm afraid I don't know her name. Wait a minute. Mrs. McMahon with her dog, and Cecil Skinner's girl, I don't recall her name either right now. They came up about the same time as the ambulance."

"How about Harry?"

"Harry?" Johnson turned to Townsend. "Harry, you were there, weren't you?" He faced back to Peabody. "I'm sorry. I guess we did talk to each other but I was so caught up in what was going on with Steph, I didn't really pay attention to him. Sorry, Harry."

"Mr. Townsend?" Peabody repeated the question.

"Yes, I, I had just come out of the office when I heard shouting. But I didn't see anything. And I didn't see anybody except for who Mel just told you about."

"How about anybody else on the green, maybe moving away from everyone else?"

They both shook their heads.

Getty asked his question. "Did either of you see anybody pick up anything or get rid of anything while you were there?"

Johnson frowned and shook his head. Townsend paused for just a second, then said, "No."

Johnson cocked his head to one side. "Surely this is the work of the same person who killed Grace, isn't it? And that couldn't have been anyone there."

Peabody studied the both of them for a moment. Apparently, word hadn't gotten around town as quickly as the police department had thought. He could understand these two men not being in the loop for immediate sordid news, but he was surprised Sherri Northrup hadn't already heard and shared it with them.

"Right now, we have reason to believe that this is a different person. I'm sorry I can't share any more with you than that, I know how close you both were to Grace Mathison, but you may be hearing some news on that front very soon. But Officer Reasoner's attacker is someone else."

"Really?" Johnson was startled. "You know who Grace's killer is?" Townsend's mouth dropped open.

"I am sorry. I can't tell you any more at this time."

"Oh, my God." Johnson gripped the arms of his chair tightly. Townsend couldn't say anything, but his pen was clicking madly. In and out, in and out.

Peabody asked, "Is there anything else you might be able to tell us?"

They both shook their heads slowly. "No, no, nothing else," Johnson said, even more slowly.

Peabody stood up with Getty closing his notebook and following. "Thank you, gentlemen. We appreciate your assistance and your time."

Townsend stood up slowly and shook their hands this time, but

Johnson didn't rise.

Peabody and Getty walked through the outer office to hear Sherri Northrup on the phone. "You don't say! I wouldn't have believed it! No! It can't be him!" She didn't even notice their passing. Peabody guessed the other men would be hearing the news now.

They went through the door and turned left towards the bank.

"Any thoughts?" Peabody asked.

"Both of them appeared pretty shook up, both by Officer Reasoner's stabbing, and by the news that it's a different suspect than for Mrs. Mathison."

"Yes, but they were both very close to Mrs. Mathison. You might not be aware, but Townsend was her nephew, and Mel Johnson was her – I guess you would call it sometime boyfriend. And they both had talked with Stephanie just yesterday afternoon.

"I'm also talking about Mel barely noticing Townsend last night. Did Townsend just show up at the end? Where was he before that?"

They arrived at the bank and opened the front door. Peabody nodded to the security guard, Teddy Witherspoon, just inside the door and walked to one of the teller's windows.

"Good morning, how can I help you?" It was the cheeriest greeting he expected to get today.

"Yes, I need to see the manager, Charlene Matthews."

The teller looked to her left, to a glassed-in office. They could see Matthews in there on the phone. The bank manager glanced up at that moment, saw who was standing at the counter, and apparently said good-bye to whoever was on the other end of the line, hanging up the phone. She stood up and came out to greet them.

"Officer Peabody, good morning. I assume you're here about last night."

"Yes, I am, Mrs. Matthews. If I could ask you a few questions?"

"Certainly, whatever you need. Come into my office. Cheryl," she spoke to the teller, "I'm going to be with these gentlemen, so I am not to be disturbed."

She closed the door, and they sat down. Peabody introduced Getty for what seemed like the umpteenth time that morning. Matthews nodded, but made no comment.

"Mrs. Matthews, you were coming out of the bank last night when Officer Reasoner was attacked, is that right?"

"Yes, sir, I had just locked up the front door, when I heard…a yell, I guess it was. I turned and saw Chief Pierson and Officer Addams running toward a shadow on the ground. I couldn't tell what it was from that distance. The chief was coming from the bandstand, and Officer Addams appeared to be running from the direction of the station."

"Do you always come out the front door? Don't you park around back?" Getty interjected.

Matthews appeared to redden slightly. "I am parked in the rear, but I only go out that way in bad weather. I have to turn our front sign to *Closed,* and I have to admit I like to look out on the green at dusk. It gives me comfort at the end of the day."

"And did you see anything out on the green last night?" Peabody asked.

"I'm afraid I hadn't gotten that far, Officer. I had just locked the door and saw Mr. Peters in front of his store."

"Nobody else?"

"Not immediately. Then the yell, and as I started walking toward the commotion, Mel Johnson was also coming over and Cheryl Levinsky, one of my tellers, came from behind the building. She had been leaving too, but had gone out the back." Matthews pointed to the young woman at the front counter. "That's her out there now."

"Anybody show up later?"

Matthews sat back and looked up at the ceiling in thought.

"Mr. Johnson's employee, Harry Townsend, I think his name is." She looked down at Peabody. "They were both here with Officer Reasoner yesterday. To get into Mrs. Mathison's safety deposit box." She paused and took a chocolate from a bowl at the corner of her desk. Peabody looked at the bowl. They were small individually wrapped candy bars, the kind the company likes to call "Fun-Size". But Peabody thought they were only "Fun-Size" if you find unwrapping five of them "Fun". Because that's how many it took to make a regular sized bar. She saw him looking at the bowl.

"Would you care for one, Officer? And you, Officer Getty?"

Peabody put a hand in the bowl and surreptitiously palmed two. Getty took only one. "Thank you."

"Mrs. McMahon was there with her Pekingese. She walks her every night just as we close, regular as clockwork. Though I suspect Mrs. McMahon needs the regularity more than the dog. And the Skinner girl, I don't know her first name. She sometimes goes to the Corner Grocery to meet her father as he gets off work. And I think they sometimes get an ice cream at The Dairy Bar on the other corner. I don't recall anybody else. Oh, till Mayor Plummer showed up, just about the same time as the ambulance." She shook her head. "If there was anybody else, I couldn't tell you who it was."

Peabody looked at Getty, who took his cue to ask his question. "Did you see anybody pick up or get rid of anything at any time?"

Matthews shrugged. "There was a lot going on by then. And my attention, all our attention was focused on Officer Reasoner. I'm sorry, that's all I can tell you."

Peabody balled up the candy wrappers together, so they looked like one. "Thank you, Mrs. Matthews. Now I'd like to ask you about yesterday afternoon when Officer Reasoner was here with Johnson and Townsend. Did you notice anything in particular at that time?"

Matthews picked up a paper clip and tapped it against the desk. "No, nothing in particular. I mean, I do get asked to get into the safety deposit boxes of the deceased, but not usually with the police present. That was different. Mr. Townsend seemed nervous, but his aunt had just died. I wouldn't expect him to act normally. But then, I don't know what his 'normal' behavior would be. Maybe he's just a nervous person.

"I opened the box for them, then left the room. I assume they talked, but I don't listen in on these conversations. However, Officer Reasoner did ask me to make copies of everything when they were done. That's not typical. I did not look at any specifics of anything, but they appeared to be the normal types of things that are kept in these boxes – wills, insurance papers, receipts. Nothing of a criminal nature, if that's what you're wondering."

Peabody stood up and held out his hand.

"Thank you again. You have been most helpful."

"You are welcome. Let me know if I can help with anything else."

He paused. "Actually, now that you mention it, could we talk with

Cheryl, is it? Since she was also there last night."

"Of course. You can use my office." Matthews went out, and Peabody sat back down, taking the opportunity to put several "Fun-Size" bars in his pocket.

Cheryl Levinsky closed the door behind her and looked anxiously at the officers until Peabody gestured for her to take the seat behind the desk. "This is your chance to take the seat of power," he said. She giggled. "Hi, I am Officer Peabody, and this is Officer Getty."

She gave a small wave and said, "Hi."

"We just wanted to ask if you had seen or heard anything last night on the green."

"You mean when that policewoman was stabbed? Oh, no, I got there after it happened." She was directing her attention and answers to Getty. That seemed to be happening with the younger women. "I was out back and heard yelling, so I ran around front, but I just saw a group of people standing there watching the policemen."

"Do you know who was in the group?" Getty asked.

"Well, Mrs. Matthews, of course. And Mr. Peters from the hardware store. They're usually out front together. I think the two men from next door, but I don't know their names. Unless they're Johnson and Johnson? And then the mayor came from his other office across the green, you know where I mean?" They both nodded, but she only looked at Getty's. "And a couple of other people, but I don't know who they were. An older lady with a dog and a young girl."

"Did you see anybody pick anything up or get rid of anything?"

"Nope, er, no sir. By the time I could figure out what was going on, the ambulance came up, making a lot of noise, then there were people rushing around, shouting things. Some of the people watching started wandering a little bit, but I didn't pay particular attention. I did see the two policemen and the mayor walk back over to the police department after the ambulance left. I started to go over to ask Mrs. Matthews if she knew what had happened, but she was whispering with Mr. Peters. The insurance men were talking with each other. The others were leaving, so I went around back and drove away. That was it."

Peabody rolled up another candy bar wrapper, which no one had seen him take, and said, "Thank you, Ms. Levinsky. If you think of anything else, be sure to let us know."

She nodded at Peabody and smiled at Getty, then opened the door and left. Peabody and Getty looked at each other, then followed her out.

Getty approached the security guard. "Teddy, don't suppose you were around last night?"

"No, George, I only work till two. Jed Will, the other guard, comes in then, but he only works through the after-work rush and the locking-up, then he clocks out about a half-hour before Mrs. Matthews leaves." He shrugged. "Sorry."

Peabody clapped him on the shoulder. "That's okay, Teddy, have a good day."

# CHAPTER 21

Addams was not particularly enjoying his current conversation with Sharon Alvarez, the district attorney, so he turned most of his nonverbal attention to the pretty assistant DA, Gail Whittier. They had met at a few social gatherings with mutual friends, and he sensed there just might be some chemistry there, though now was not the time to pursue it.

He had returned to the department from the Mathison house to find Mike Wannamaker anxiously sitting with Alvarez and Whittier, waiting for the return of anybody so that Mike could get on with almost anything else. Talking with any member of the legal profession had never been his strong suit.

"Bud, I got a call regarding some graffiti behind the Church of Hope and Light. Pastor Johns wants someone to look at it before they clean it up. Apparently, it's a little, uh, personal about one of the congregation. So he doesn't want it up too long, doesn't want anybody else to see it. But I was waiting because I thought somebody should be here, seeing as how we have a prisoner. And a couple of people who needed to see him." Wannamaker shifted his eyes to the attorneys.

"Yeah, Mike, go take care of it. I'll be here for a little while anyway. Hopefully, one of the Gettys or George will be back soon."

"Great. I shouldn't be gone too long. When I'm done, I can bring something back for lunch from Mac's. You want anything?"

"Uh, yeah. A meatloaf sandwich from Mac's will be fine. I don't care what kind."

"Sounds good. I might get one too. Maybe with fried onions." Wannamaker went out the back door, starting to whistle now that he was free from having to entertain the legal profession.

Addams turned toward the two women waiting for him, one patiently and smilingly, the senior one not so much.

"Now, Ms. Alvarez, Miss Whittier, what can I do for you? Have you had a chance to talk with Jeff yet?"

Whittier smiled a little at the "Miss" reference. In their last conversation, she had been "Gail". Alvarez stood, but without a smile.

"Yes, we have, thank you. Mr. Laurenfeld just left, and we have Chief Pierson's story about what has happened. We need to talk about how we are going to proceed from this point."

"Okay, how about if we go into Conference Room A?"

She pointed in a different direction. "We could use the Chief's office. It's a little more out of the way, Chief, and it is yours now."

It took Addams a second to realize that, since he was now Chief, it was his room to use. This was going to take some getting used to.

As they went into the room, Whittier smiled at him again and said, "Good to see you again, Marty." It lifted his spirits, but not enough and not for long.

Now, after sharing information and personal opinions, Addams and Alvarez disagreed about whether to pursue Pierson as a suspect in the attack on Officer Reasoner or not.

"Chief Pierson is known to have a motive," Alvarez pointed out. "Officer Reasoner had just accused him of killing Grace Mathison. He was there at the scene at the time. He was the closest to her in regards to proximity. He admitted it was his fault."

"But his motive is gone with his confession immediately following the incident. And I saw him running toward her, not away from her." Addams rubbed his forehead. "It would have been a neat trick for him to have run thirty feet away then turn right around and run back to her."

"Maybe it was to get rid of the weapon."

"We searched the area. There is no weapon, certainly not within the range that he could have gone. His comment about it being his fault most likely had to do with Mathison's death and with creating the whole situation in the first place. With Officer Reasoner simply being in that place at that time."

"But we can't just dismiss him," Alvarez insisted. "He was there and, without him, there is no other motive."

"Yes, as a matter of fact, there just may be." Addams pushed the copy of the home improvement receipts from the safety deposit box in front of the DA. She picked it up and scanned it.

"What? What is there?" Whittier couldn't read the paper from her seat. Alvarez raised an eyebrow in question at Addams.

He pointed to the top line of the paper. "There was an additional hidden room put on that house about fifteen years ago. We opened that room this morning and guess what was in it?"

"I'm not in the business of guessing," Alvarez responded sternly.

Addams held up a hand. "I'm sorry. It was meant to be a rhetorical question. The contents of that room appear to be stolen property from several robberies around this area."

He leaned even further forward. "We believe that whoever attacked Stephanie had reason to fear that she was going to find out about that room since she had made this copy to bring back here and study. The crime scene unit from Oldstown is going over that room right now, and Officer Getty is going through the inventory, comparing it to lists of reported stolen items from houses around the town. Now that may be a plausible motive." The "we believe" may have been a little presumptive. Addams had just come up with the theory on the spot. Having made his point, he sat back.

Alvarez put the paper down. "Okay, you may have something there. But you still have to tie this in with the actual assault on Officer Reasoner. And with more than a guess that she may have possibly suspected the existence of this room."

There was a knock on the door. Addams said, "Come in" and the door opened. Marie Hazlett stood there.

"Marie, I didn't know you were back. Any..." He swallowed in anxious concern. "Anything new on Steph?"

She shook her head. "No, it's still the same. But her parents wanted me back here to help – to help figure out what happened." Hazlett looked at Alvarez. "For starters, they don't believe Jeff had anything to do with it." Alvarez' stern expression did not change.

"Thank you, Marie. I appreciate your being here." Addams said.

"I also wanted to let you know that George and Seth have returned. But Seth went right back out. He said he wanted to check on something, be back in a few minutes. And," she handed him a piece of paper, "we got some information from where Harry Townsend used to work. They were slow in responding to our initial request two days ago."

Addams held the paper, but continued to look at Hazlett. "Yes?"

"It seems that it was suggested that he leave his previous employment. They said he was a good worker, but they suspected that he had been stealing from the store." She again turned toward Alvarez and Whittier. "He worked as the manager of the electrical appliance department at a department store." Then back to Addams. "Nothing was ever proven, but both the store and Townsend felt it was in everyone's best interests for him to leave. That apparently is when he came here."

Whittier asked, "What kinds of things were missing?"

Hazlett looked at Addams, and he nodded.

"Mostly items from the appliances. Televisions and stereo equipment. Also some jewelry and watches. Not a lot, but enough to suspect somebody from the inside."

Alvarez asked Addams, "That match what you found?"

He nodded. "That's exactly the types of property that was in the hidden closet."

Alvarez picked up the list of home repairs. "This closet was installed, what, fifteen years ago? So this sounds like something that has been going on for a while." She waved the paper at Addams. "I think we now do have a legitimate motive and a legitimate suspect. Do we know if anyone saw him at the scene last night?"

Addams shook his head. "I don't know. I don't specifically recall him there, but then, that wasn't where my attention was. Officer Peabody has been out trying to find out who was seen then."

Alvarez stood up. "I understand Officer Peabody has returned. Maybe it's time for us to reconvene in the conference room and hear what he has to say from his morning's activities."

Hazlett stepped aside at the door as Alvarez breezed out of the room, followed by Whittier, who briefly touched Hazlett's arm. Addams took a deep breath and, much more slowly, rose from the chief's seat, waving for Hazlett to go ahead.

"Thanks, Marie. Perfect timing, as it happens. I think we may now have moved away from Jeff as a suspect in the assault on Steph."

At that moment, both the front and back doors opened. Mike Wannamaker pushed through the back door carrying a big bag in one hand and a carrier of drinks in another. He saw Addams and held them up. Addams pointed to Conference Room A, and Wannamaker walked in that direction. Peabody, who had been perusing a plate of pecan rolls in the outer offices, saw the *Mac's Café* logo on the side of the bag and came along with him, apparently changing his mind for the moment about the rolls.

Through the front door came Seth Getty holding three big blue trash bags. Addams waited for him while everyone else entered the conference room.

"What do you have, Seth?"

"It occurred to me during the interviews this morning, that last night several people were milling about in front of those businesses. From the interviews, nobody saw anyone throw anything away or try to hide anything, but we haven't found a weapon." He held up the trash bags. "There were two trash bins along the sidewalk in that area and one on the other side of the park that hadn't been emptied yet, and I thought it might not even register consciously to see someone throw something in a trash can. It's just such a natural occurrence that no one thinks anything of it. So," he shrugged, "I thought I should check it out."

Addams clapped him on the shoulder.

"Good idea, Seth. Bring them in here with us. Hopefully, they won't smell too bad. I'll let you take the bags to the other side of the room and start looking through them while we find out what you and George learned this morning."

# CHAPTER 22

Addams found Wannamaker at the head of the table sorting out the sandwiches and drinks with everybody else taking seats down the sides. Seth Getty had moved to the far end of the room where there was an open area and had found some old newspapers to spread on the floor. He pulled on latex gloves, preparing to dump the trash and do the sorting. Addams hoped there wasn't too much of an offending odor to any of the garbage.

"How did the graffiti investigation go, Mike?"

Wannamaker shrugged. "Dennis Johns is pretty sure he knows who did it. It was some obscenities on the side of their shed in back of the church. The custodian was already there ready to repaint it. The pastor just wanted it documented in case it keeps happening. He'll deal with it, and he's not looking for us to do anything yet. He'd rather keep the name of the guilty party to himself right now. I'm sure he can address 'guilt' pretty well."

Addams nodded. "Good, if the pastor feels comfortable with handling it, we've got enough going on."

"Okay." Wannamaker held up two sandwiches toward the rest of the group. "I've got six meatloaves and two grilled cheese. And a large bag of Mac's special onion rings. I had no idea who was going to be here and what they might want. All of the drinks are Marge's Peach Lemonade. It's hard to go wrong with that. And too bad if you wanted tea."

Hazlett took one of the grilled cheeses, and Alvarez asked if there was a spicy chili meatloaf. The rest took whatever was handy, but Peabody pulled the bag holding the extra unclaimed grilled cheese a little bit closer to his seat. Getty put his sandwich aside for the moment – "I'll get it later." Addams was glad Peabody was down at that end of the table with Getty and the trash. His appetite never seemed to be disturbed by anything.

Once all the food was passed out, and everybody had started eating,

Addams stood in front of the board. It still included all the notes from investigating Mrs. Mathison's death, but he wasn't up to erasing them yet. He twirled it over to a blank board on the other side, and Marie Hazlett moved up to start taking a new set of notes under the heading of *Officer Reasoner's Attack.*

"Okay. I'm going to start by sharing what we know so far. Jeff has confessed to the apparently accidental death of Mrs. Mathison. His statement is consistent with the evidence that we have found and with the probability of it being an accident. He is currently under arrest and in Cell One because his actions did lead to a death and then he interfered with the evidence and the investigation.

"After confronting him at the bandstand last night with what she had deduced, Steph walked away from him into the trees and the dusk and was stabbed. This we know. She is presently in critical condition at Memorial Hospital. As Jeff has admitted to Mrs. Mathison's death, which removes his motive, we knew we must have a brand new assailant not connected to the first assault." He carefully avoided looking at District Attorney Alvarez.

"Through paperwork from the Mathison safety deposit box and statements from Emmett Doolittle, her yard man, we have discovered a hidden closet in the house that contains miscellaneous electronics, jewelry, and so on, that appear to be stolen items from garage and yard sales. Sam Getty and Phil Culbertson are going through those now to confirm that."

Seth looked up surprised, and Peabody almost dropped his sandwich. Almost but he caught it again. This was the first they had heard about the hidden room and its contents.

"Marie has also received information from Harry Townsend's previous employer that he had been encouraged to leave that job because of suspicions regarding him stealing exactly the types of items found in the closet."

"Oh my." Peabody laid down the sandwich and sat up straighter in his seat. "Grace Mathison was hiding stolen goods for her nephew?"

"Don't jump to conclusions." Alvarez felt the need to admonish. "Though, if one were impelled to jump, there are worse directions."

Addams took control of the discussion again. "So, we have an assault specifically directed at Officer Stephanie Reasoner. She was the last one in the house yesterday afternoon. She may or may not have suspected an issue with the size of the spare room, but she did make copies of the papers from the safety deposit box and was planning on studying them, which would have led her to that secret room."

Getty interrupted from the far end of the room. "But would she have pursued it once she suspected Chief Pierson of the first death? I don't know her, but wouldn't that have closed down the case and she might never have looked at the papers at all?"

Addams smiled slightly. "That's a good question, Seth. That's a really good point. Which means that her assailant would not have known that Jeff caused Grace's death and that the investigation could have been ending."

He turned to Peabody, who had apparently regained his appetite and was in the midst of reaching for another onion ring. "George, what did you and Seth learn?"

"Well." He wiped his hands on a napkin. "We first went to see Judy Pierson and get the box of objects that Jeff had taken from the Mathison house. It was just like he said, including a bowling trophy with what appeared to be blood sort of wiped off of it. We dropped the box off to Mike here at the station. We wanted it out of our hands." He shook his head. "I don't want to do anything like that talking with Judy again. That was rough."

"Sorry to interrupt." Getty's voice came up from the floor beyond the end of the table.

"But I have a knife here, from the bin across the green."

Into the sudden silence, with two latexed fingers, he held up what appeared to be a camping knife, then peered closely at it. "There appears to be some sort of fancy design or lettering on the end of the handle. I can't quite make out what it is. It's pretty small." He laid it on that end of the table, on top of Peabody's napkin.

Peabody pulled his chair closer to it, and Alvarez jumped up to move down the table to look at it for herself.

Addams whispered to Hazlett, "There's no way Jeff could have gotten across the green to drop that there. That should definitely eliminate him from Alvarez's mind."

"I think it's fancy initials," Peabody muttered. "But doggone if I can tell what they are yet. All these crazy unreadable letters they make these days. Stylized, I think they call it. Not what I was taught in school."

Alvarez looked up. "I think there may be blood on the edge. There was probably a quick wipe, but it didn't get it all. And I can't tell clearly from the letter style either. I could hazard a guess, but I'd rather not at this point. Is there a jeweler or somebody in town that would be able to identify these styles?"

Addams nodded. "There's Hansfelder's in the next block. I know they do a lot of engraving."

Hazlett was already out the door heading to the phone.

"And, Marie," he called out. "See if Phil can come look at this knife." He turned back to Getty. "Anything else?"

Getty set a handkerchief on the table next to the knife. "This looks like it has blood on it, but it came from a trashcan on this side of the street. I'll keep on looking if there's anything more."

"Okay, we'll give that to Phil too, and the box George and Seth got from the Pierson's garage. And anything else you come up with. Seth, good idea to get those trash cans."

Addams faced the rest of the table. "This is a big find. Under the circumstances, it would be hard to believe that it's not the weapon used on Stephanie. However, if the handkerchief is tied to it, that is probably what was used to wipe it down, hoping to erase any fingerprints. We'll let Emil Hansfelder and Phil Culbertson look at them and see what they can tell us.

"George, anything more for us?"

At some point, the extra grilled cheese had disappeared. George opened Seth Getty's notebook and flipped through a few pages. "I think we're pretty clear on who was there last night. Charlene Matthews, Hank Peters, Mel Johnson, Harry Townsend, Cheryl Levinsky, who also works at the bank, JJ Plummer, Mrs. McMahon, her dog, and Tracy Skinner, Cecil's daughter. We interviewed everybody except JJ, Mrs. McMahon, Tracy, and Mrs. McMahon's dog. JJ and Mrs. McMahon are coming into the station early this afternoon, but we can't get Tracy till after school."

He reported some of the specifics from the interviews, but concluded, "So far nobody has seen anything useful. They all heard a yell, or something, but nobody saw anybody near Steph except for Jeff and Bud running to her.

The only significant thing is that they all sort of agreed that they didn't see Harry at first and they don't know when he got there or where he exactly came from. But it was after everybody else."

He set the notebook down. "Like Seth said, they didn't see anybody drop anything or throw anything like a knife away, even into a waste can."

Addams nodded. "No eyewitness, but that was always a long shot. We know who was in the area immediately afterward, but it could have been somebody that took off on the other side of the green. However, that wouldn't explain the handkerchief on this side, and..." He looked around the room.

"And, our prime suspect was there, but late. Somebody that could have gone across the green and deposited the knife in that trash can and come back. Harry Townsend was with Steph in the house and the bank, and he may have heard her say something that made him think she was going to find out about that room. He has a history that ties in with these goods found in the house."

Addams pointed at Wannamaker and Getty. "Seth, you had a good look at that knife. I want you to go over to the Mathison house and see if she has any silverware or cutlery that matches that design. Maybe we'll get lucky, and there's a missing knife from one of those knife blocks. Mike, I hate to ask you this, but I'd rather have you at the station. Can you finish going through the trash there?"

Seth stood up and started to take his gloves off, then seemed to realize he may still need them at the house. He left the room. Wannamaker pulled on a new set of gloves and took Seth's place, kneeling on the floor.

Marie Hazlett came back into the room as Seth Getty was leaving. "Emil Hansfelder is on his way. So is Phil. And several items in that closet match the list of stolen goods from garage and yard sales, as well as many of the smaller items on Mrs. Mathison's shelves. Since they have already taken pictures and Crime Scene has done their thing, Sam is going to start moving the items to here."

Alvarez stood. Whittier decided that meant that she needed to stand too.

"Chief, I think it's time to make an arrest." Alvarez declared. "There's definitely cleaning up that needs to be done, but I think we've got more than enough to at least arrest Harry Townsend on theft charges. And to ask for his 'assistance' in the attack on Officer Reasoner. I will take care of the warrants, including one to search his residence." She looked around. "Anything else that we haven't specifically covered yet? No? Okay, get to it."

She left the room. Whittier, after giving Addams a rueful smile, followed her.

George glanced at his watch. "The mayor and Mrs. McMahon will be coming in, but probably not for another hour. After this, I don't think they have much more to add."

Addams stood and looked down at the sandwich that he had barely touched. He had the sense that this was the way for many meals from now on.

"George, you're with me. I think you and I need to be the ones making this arrest. Marie, you and Mike have the office. And if our witnesses come in early, tell them we'll be back soon. In fact, Mike could start talking with them. You know what to ask, Mike."

# CHAPTER 23

Addams and Peabody found Sherri Northrup at her desk, but on the phone. "Yes, I know. It's getting so you can't trust anyone anymore. In Summerfield, of all places. Uh-oh, I've got more police coming in, Lisha, and I don't think it's to buy a new policy. I gotta go."

She hung up and turned to them. "Well, Officer Addams, I think that makes the whole force that has come through in the last couple of days." She softened her tone and addressed Peabody. "George, how's Steph?"

"The same, Sherri, the same. Nothing new." He inclined his head towards the back offices. "Mr. Townsend still back there?"

"Oh, yes. And Mr. Johnson. And I don't think they're doing anything. Mr. Johnson had a client earlier today. Old man Haversham seems to have a question every week about his homeowner's policy. Does it cover this kind of leak? What if this happens? Oh my, I probably shouldn't be telling you any of this. But you are the police. It's still confidential, isn't it?"

Addams was already moving. "Thank you, Sherri, I think Officer Peabody knows the way."

Harry Townsend had heard the voices and had come to the door. "Hello, gentlemen. Has something else happened? Or is this a follow-up to earlier?" The pen was clicking, clicking in his left hand. He backed into the room and waved to the chairs in front of the desk.

"Take a seat, Officers Peabody and, Addams, isn't it?"

Peabody corrected him. "It's Chief Addams, now."

Townsend's eyebrows rose. "Really? I had heard there were probably some changes coming. I'd say congratulations, but I don't think the circumstances really call for it." He moved to his seat behind the desk. "I do want to let you know that I don't personally hate Chief Pierson for what he did. I hate what he did, and I may never forgive him, but, from what I've heard, it was more of an accident than anything deliberate.”

Addams cleared his throat and spoke. “We’re not here to sit, Mr. Townsend. We are here to arrest you on charges of theft, specifically the items found in your aunt’s secret closet, and to also bring you in for questioning regarding the attempted murder, at this point, of Officer Stephanie Reasoner.”

Townsend sat down hard, but continued to click his pen. “I, I don’t understand. A secret closet? What closet? What, what items? I didn’t attack Stephanie. It wasn’t me.”

Addams simply stared at him, and Townsend stopped talking.

“Officer Peabody.”

Peabody went around the desk and gingerly pulled Townsend back out of the seat, turning him around to put handcuffs on.

“Harry, don’t say anything.” A voice came from the doorway. “I’ll get you a lawyer. Don’t say another word.”

Addams turned to Mel Johnson, who was now standing there. Peabody started reading his rights to the now silent Townsend.

“Mr. Johnson.” Addams nodded to him.

“Bud, I heard George say you’re now chief. But I don’t know what you’re doing here. Harry wouldn’t have hurt anybody, least of all Stephanie. That’s not in his nature.”

“We’ll see. But that’s not the only issue. We have found a secret room in Mrs. Mathison’s house, full of objects stolen from around the community. And with enough evidence to arrest Mr. Townsend here. And that’s all I can tell you. Any other conversation will have to be with his attorney.”

With his rights having been completed, Townsend started up again. “But it wasn’t me. I didn’t attack anybody. Really, it wasn’t me. I wasn’t even there. Tell them, Mel.”

Johnson sighed deeply. “Don’t say anything, Harry. I know you didn’t do it. I’ll get you a lawyer as soon as I can. The office will pay for it. Don’t worry about it.”

As Peabody led Townsend out of the office, Johnson waved a hand for Addams to stay. “Bud...”

“Mel, we have to take him in. We have found a weapon that was probably used in the attack. We’re checking now on where it came from.

But even without that, we have a secret closet at Mrs. Mathison's that is filled with merchandise that has been stolen from around town. We have information that Harry Townsend was suspected of theft in his previous job. Somehow all that stuff got into the house, and we just can't see Grace Mathison doing it by herself. Can you?"

"No, no." Johnson shook his head.

"I shouldn't be telling you all this, but I know you've got a stake in everything that's been going on. You'd better get that attorney."

Addams turned and followed the other two to the reception area. Sherri Northrup's mouth was open, but, for once, no sounds were coming out.

"Sherri." Johnson was trying to get her attention, but she wasn't responding, just staring as Peabody and Townsend went out the door. "Sherri." He knocked on her desk. "Sherri!"

She finally turned.

"Get me Matt Laurenfeld. Tell him it's an emergency." He started back to his office, muttering, "This has all gone to crap."

Addams finally went out after the other two, letting the door swing shut behind him.

# CHAPTER 24

George Peabody took Harry Townsend back to the cells while Martin Addams walked slowly back into the chief's office. Cell One was already occupied by Jeff Pierson, and, after hesitating for just a moment, Peabody placed Townsend two cells away, in Cell Three, and took off the handcuffs.

Pierson stood. "What's going on, Pops? It's getting crowded in here."

"You know how Grace Mathison had those small curio things from all those garage sales thefts?" Pierson nodded. "Of course you do. Well, apparently we've found the bigger things, the appliances, jewelry, electronics, in a hidden closet at the Mathison house in a back bedroom. And it looks like Harry here probably is the primary culprit. Isn't that right, Harry?"

Harry grabbed the bars. "Look, I told you, I had nothing to do with stabbing Officer Reasoner. I don't know who did that, but it wasn't me."

"What?" Pierson also took hold of his bars. "You think he did that too?"

Peabody came over to Pierson. "We think Stephanie had reason to think there was something odd about the size of that room and that she let him know what she was thinking. Which would have given him a reason to stop her. We're following up on a few things, but we're pretty sure that he was involved in the thefts."

"Yes, yes!" Townsend yelled down the corridor. "I will admit to the stuff in the closet, but I didn't attack her. I didn't do that. I wouldn't try to kill someone!" He pleaded directly to Pierson.

Peabody and Pierson looked at each other. Peabody calmly said, "Mr. Townsend, I think you better wait for your lawyer."

Townsend and Pierson now stared at each other across the empty cell in between. Peabody turned and left the hall.

On his way back to the outer offices, Peabody passed Conference Room

A and through the window on the door saw Addams and Wannamaker talking with Mrs. McMahon, with her Pekingese on her lap. Apparently, she didn't go anywhere without that dog.

———   ———   ———

"Mrs. McMahon," Wannamaker was taking the lead in the questions. She had known him as the previous chief, but probably wasn't yet aware of Addams' new status. "We appreciate your taking the time to come in to see us."

"Of course, of course. It's my duty. I have always tried to help the police. It's our civic responsibility, isn't it, Fifi?" She caressed the dog's head.

"Fifi? Really?" Addams hadn't meant to say it out loud.

"Not Fifirealy. It's really Fifirello, but she knows I only use her whole name when I'm mad at her. But that's not very often, is it sweetie?" The dog didn't really look like she cared, but she was comfortable.

"Mrs. McMahon, we understand you were at the town green last night when Officer Reasoner was attacked." Wannamaker returned to the purpose of the interview.

"Oh, it wasn't when she was attacked. It must have been right afterward. The ambulance was already there."

"Thank you. Right afterward. We have a list of the people that we know were there." Wannamaker showed her the list. "Can you think of anyone else? Anyone that may have been there for only a minute or so?"

She perused the list for a moment. "No, no, that seems to be about right. I only saw Mayor Plummer and Officer Addams," she tilted her head in his direction, "from a distance, as they were walking back to the station with Chief Pierson. Nobody else."

"Did you notice anything else happen? Anybody running away? Anyone throw anything away or pick anything up?"

"I did see that young man from Mel Johnson's office put something in the waste can near the corner. I don't know what it was, but it must have been small. It fit in one hand."

Addams sat up. "Something small? Could it have been a handkerchief?"

"I don't know, Officer Addams. I wasn't that close, and I wasn't really paying attention to him, you know. He went over and talked to Mel Johnson right after that. Maybe Mel knows what he threw away." She looked from one policeman to the other. "Is there anything else, officers? Fifi gets nervous if she's in a strange place for very long. And you never know what she may do when she's nervous." Fifi did not look either nervous or as if she was about to do anything.

"No, thank you, Mrs. McMahon. If you think of anything else, will you let us know?"

She nodded and said, "Of course," stood up, and carried Fifi out of the room. "Yes, you're okay. We're going home now. Don't you worry." The officers followed her out to the main office.

JJ Plummer was in the outer area telling Marie Hazlett, "I'll be just next door. You can give a call when they're ready, and I'll be back." But then he turned and saw Addams and Wannamaker. "Oh, never mind. It looks like they are ready for me now." He strode over and shook their hands.

"Gentlemen. I don't really think that there's anything I can add, but I do understand the need for us to do this, to ensure that we have all the facts. Should we do this in your office, Bud?"

Addams paused. "I think we better do it in the conference room. Just to keep our procedures consistent. Do you mind?"

"Of course not. No sense of any improprieties. I understand perfectly. Lead the way."

Though Addams did intend to lead the way and had made the decision as to which room, he wondered if it seemed as if the mayor was still in charge.

"Oh, Bud." Hazlett held out an envelope for him before he turned to leave. "Emil Hansfelder was here and took a look at our...piece of evidence. This is his opinion regarding the engraving. Seth has reported that there was nothing in Mrs. Mathison's house that matched that engraving or anything like it at all. And we now have the search warrants that we need."

"Thank you, Marie. Have the Gettys start on those searches. Everybody else is busy at the moment." He took the envelope, and they crossed to the conference room.

"Take a seat, Mayor."

"JJ, Bud, please. You're the police chief now. We're equals, both employed by the city."

"JJ." Both Addams and Wannamaker sat. "Well, what can you tell us about last night? What you saw or heard. Anything you might have noticed." Addams pulled a piece of paper out of the envelope and read it while Plummer talked.

"As I told you, I pretty much saw what you saw. I heard a shout or a yell, some sort of loud verbal noise. I was inside my office, but with the window open. I thought it could have been anything – children playing, somebody yelling across the green. I did look out, and that's when I saw some figures running. Apparently, that was you and Jeff. I didn't know that at the time, but I thought, well, maybe I had better go see what was happening. At first, it didn't appear to be urgent, so I spent just a moment closing up the office, but then I saw the emergency squad arrive and I hurried across the green."

"JJ, tell us who you saw when you got there," Wannamaker asked.

"As soon as I got close, I saw Bud and Jeff. And Jim McGarry, the EMT. I went over to stand out of the way with the other people until the ambulance left. There were Hank Peters, and Charlene Matthews, and Mel Johnson. Mel's associate, I believe his name is Townsend. And a young woman from the bank, Cheryl Levinsky. I don't believe there was anyone else. Oh yes, except Mrs. McMahon and her dog, Fifi, who came up after I did." Addams was surprised that the mayor knew the dog's name, but then he was a politician. "And Cecil Skinner's daughter, Tracy or Stacy." Apparently, the girl didn't vote yet.

"Yes, that's pretty much what we've gotten from everybody else. They were mostly there when you got there?"

"Yes, except for Luellen McMahon and the Skinner girl."

Addams interrupted. "You started from the other side of the green. Did you see anybody on the green, either coming or going?"

"Not anybody in particular. I have the impression that as I was starting to cross the street, there was a figure hurrying across farther north of me. But that's just an impression. I couldn't swear to it."

"Did you see anyone throw anything away? Into a trashcan or onto the ground?"

"No, that wasn't where my attention was. I wasn't watching them. I was looking at you and Stephanie, though I didn't really know that was who it was at the time."

Addams held up the note from the envelope.

"Mayor, JJ…" He breathed out. "We have found a knife in the trashcan on the east side of the green. Officer Getty, I forget which one at the moment, searched them and came back with the contents. We have reason to think that this knife might be the weapon used to attack Stephanie. There were stylized initials on its hilt. They have been identified by Emil Hansfelder of Hansfelder Jewelers as two capital Js. JJ. As in JJ Plummer."

Wannamaker looked startled. Addams leaned forward and looked into Plummer's eyes. "JJ, do you have any knives with your initials engraved on them?"

"No, Bud. No, I don't." Plummer answered steadily, but shifted in his seat. "I do have a few things…hand towels, serving trays, that sort of thing – with a 'JP' on them. I'd be more likely to use the initial from my last name, just as my wife, Paula, has PP on a few of her things. That is not my knife."

Addams sighed and sat back. "It's one of the questions we have to ask – one of the things we have to pursue – JJ. I'm sure you understand. In this situation, no one seems to be just who or what we expected them to be."

Plummer waved a hand. "And you're welcome to search my house, and my office, if you want to confirm it. Though there is quite a bit of confidential material in my office. I would have to protect that. It's all paperwork though, no hidden weapons."

"Thank you for offering, Mayor. It saves us having to get a warrant. I'm afraid we're going to have to do that. We have to rule out as well as gather direct evidence." Addams didn't want the mayor to know quite yet that they already had a likely suspect in custody.

"Mike, would you accompany the mayor back to his office, both his offices, legal and mayoral, and perform that search for us? You okay with that?"

"Oh, I think I can still remember what needs to be done." Wannamaker stood up. "And don't worry, JJ, I'll be gentle."

# CHAPTER 25

As Wannamaker and Mayor Plummer left the conference room, George Peabody came up to the entrance. Addams waved him into the room, and Peabody closed the door behind him.

"Hey, Bud, anything new?"

"Mrs. McMahon saw Harry Townsend throw something in the wastebasket at the corner, but nothing else worthwhile. However, the initials on the knife have been identified as 'JJ'."

"The mayor? I don't believe it."

"Would you have believed Jeff killing Mrs. Mathison?"

"No." Peabody shook his head. "No, I would never have believed that either."

"I think we're going to have to be willing to believe almost anything at this point. Jeff's name starts with 'J' too. I don't know what his middle initial is. Maybe he's also a 'JJP', like the mayor."

"Wait a minute, we've already eliminated Jeff as a suspect...didn't we? We've got to go somewhere else."

"You're right, George. All I know for sure is that I know I didn't do it. Did you do it?"

"No! Of course not!"

"So I didn't do it. I'm trusting you didn't do it. I'm pretty sure Marie didn't do it. And, for all intents and purposes, Jeff didn't do it. That still leaves us with a lot of possibilities."

"Oh, come on. We have our suspect behind bars already. Why do we need to keep looking?"

Addams sighed. "I know, I know. Townsend makes sense for this. We have motive and opportunity. He looks good for it. But I'm trying to figure out what he is doing with a knife with 'JJ' on the handle."

Peabody shrugged. "Maybe it was one of the stolen items. Could have come from anywhere."

Addams, realizing that he should have thought of that himself, reluctantly nodded. "That's a valid point, George. Why don't you check and see if it fits the description of any stolen items? Or if Townsend has anything in his background that might go with 'JJ'...mother or maternal grandparent or something?"

"Yep, I can do that. Makes more sense to me. But I still think we've already got our man, Bud." He opened the door and left.

Addams went back to what was now his office, but he couldn't even get inside the chief's door before Marie Hazlett called to him.

"Chief!"

He was very tempted to pretend that he didn't know she meant him, but he knew he had to do what he had to do. No getting around it today. He turned to face her.

"Marie." Then he saw Matt Laurenfeld standing next to her desk and walked slowly over. "Matt, busy day for you. Which client are you here to see? We've only got the two."

"So you are the police chief, now, Bud?" They shook hands.

"Acting chief. There's nothing permanent yet."

"I was wondering what they were going to do. There was a big hole to fill." He cocked his head. "Bud, I've been asked to represent Harry Townsend. Mel Johnson hired me."

"Okay. We've been waiting for you, or a form of you, before we interviewed him. I guess it's back to Conference Room A for me. Marie, can I have that knife? I think both Mr. Townsend and Mr. Laurenfeld should see it."

She pulled it out of a locked drawer, already wrapped in a protective plastic evidence bag, and handed it to him.

Addams showed it to Laurenfeld, but didn't let him touch it. "We found this in a trash can next to the green. We think this may be the weapon used to attack Officer Reasoner."

"Do we know that this belongs to Mr. Townsend? Or is it just something that you found?"

"Good lawyer question. But I think we better address that in the context of the interview, don't you?"

Laurenfeld smiled tightly and nodded. "I'd like to see my client for just a few moments first, if I can. I know we didn't do that with Chief Pierson, but that was by his choice."

"Sure. George," he called to Peabody sitting at his desk, going through the files on stolen goods. "Can you bring Harry Townsend to Conference Room A? Thanks."

Addams returned to what he was now slowly thinking of as his office to wait and the phone rang.

"Chief?" It was Hazlett. "Phil Culbertson is on the line. He has the report on the blood from the knife."

"Thanks, Marie." The line clicked. "Yeah, Phil, this is Bud Addams. What do you have for me?"

"Bud, we did the match on the traces of blood on that knife from the trash receptacle. It is a match for Stephanie's." Addams took a deep breath and let it out. "No fingerprints on the knife and nothing we can use from the handkerchief. But the blood on it matches both the knife and Stephanie. It was what was used to wipe the knife. Apparently, the culprit thought by separating them, maybe we wouldn't find both or, even if we did, be able to put them together."

"But no way of identifying the user at this point?"

"Well, not right now. But it was a handkerchief. Which means there is very likely some trace of its owner. If it was in the pocket for more than a minute anyway. We're not at a point of using DNA testing yet, but there may be something we can match from the pocket. But we'd need a suspect to match it with. Catch someone, and we can see what we can do."

"We do have a suspect, Phil. Maybe we can come up with something. Thanks, we now do have a weapon and a personal possession of the attacker. That's more than we had a couple of hours ago."

Addams hung up and looked at the knife sitting on his desk. This was not a kitchen carving knife. It had too much of a hilt to it. And the designs on it indicated that it was more likely an individual knife, not one of a set. He had never kept a hunting or camping knife of his own, but he remembered going camping with a friend when he was a kid, and the friend's father carried something that looked like this, just in case one needed a knife for...something. The father had grown up in a time when boys were expected to carry at least a jackknife by the time they reached a certain age, and his had been the adult version, not quite a hunting knife, but a general all-purpose one that was held in a sheath on the belt.

As a matter of fact, Chief Pierson had carried one sort of like this, but his was on him and removed when he was arrested, and was thoroughly examined at the time. No initials though. But a more ornate though worn handle. This one was a prized personal possession and handy enough to use at a moment's notice. He spent a moment in thought, but, besides the chief, he couldn't recall having seen anyone else with one.

# CHAPTER 26

Addams was still sitting at his desk when Hazlett poked her head around the door frame. "Bud...Chief...Chief Bud..."

"Just Bud, Marie. Please."

"Bud, they're ready for you in the interview room." Hazlett always liked to use the correct terms for current uses – interview room today for what had been conference room or storage room on previous days.

"Thanks, Marie. Could you also get for me the handkerchief that was found? I'd appreciate it."

Addams walked into the conference, now interview room, carrying a bag holding the knife and the handkerchief, both encased in plastic evidence wrappers, in one hand and a file folder in the other. Peabody followed him, holding a tape recorder and his trusty notebook.

"Mr. Townsend, Mr. Laurenfeld. With your permission, Officer Peabody will be recording this conversation."

Townsend looked at Laurenfeld, who nodded. "It's for your protection as well as theirs. I'm here to protect your legal rights and to tell you what you should or shouldn't answer."

Peabody pressed the button, sat back, and crossed his arms. This interview was going to belong to Addams.

"Okay. Mr. Townsend, you have been given your rights, is that correct?" Addams began. "Here is a card stating those rights. Do you need to have them repeated or explained?" Townsend took the card, skimmed it, and shook his head. "And Mr. Laurenfeld is here to see that they are enforced?"

Townsend nodded this time.

"Please say both responses out loud for the recording."

"Yes, I was explained my rights and, yes, I understand them."

"All right. We have two separate situations here. We're going to first address the stolen goods found in your aunt's house. Do you have anything to say about them?"

"I, I don't know anything about any stolen goods. In my aunt's house."

"Look, we know that your attorney will have advised you to say as little as possible – that the burden of proof is on us. He is right. He will also have advised you to be as truthful as possible in your responses. So I am going to lay out what we have so far and what we are pursuing.

"First, we have information from your previous employer that you were suspected of theft from their store and that is why you are no longer working there."

Laurenfeld started to speak, but Addams held up his hand.

"I know. That is not admissible in court and you were never charged. But we're not in court right now, and I wanted to let you know where we're coming from.

"We have found the secret closet in Mrs. Mathison's home. Based on the receipts from the safety deposit box, the room has been there for several years, but we don't yet know how long it has been used to hold stolen property. We have identified the objects within it as property that has been reported as stolen. The crime scene unit is presently checking for fingerprints and any other identifying markers both on the objects and inside the closet.

"You have had frequent access to her home and witnesses have reported that she said that you brought her many of the smaller objects that she displayed in her home. Objects that have been specifically listed as stolen." Here Addams stretched the truth slightly, knowing there was no current evidence as to which of the knick-knacks had been delivered by Townsend. But he wanted to see how Townsend reacted.

Townsend looked down, picked up a pen lying on the table, and started rolling it in his hand, but did not say anything. Peabody leaned forward when Townsend had put his hand out but relaxed when he realized what he was doing.

Addams continued. "No one, and I repeat no one, believes that Mrs. Mathison stole these objects, at least not on her own. Some of the pieces were definitely too big for her to carry out. And it stretches common sense to think that there was a gang of her peers and friends, older women carrying out a series of thefts like this. Petty jewelry and doodads maybe, but not the electronics or paintings. And who would have known where to sell the items, how to get rid of them? It would have been too dangerous to try to sell them in Summerfield. Too small a town with everybody knowing everybody else. So that pretty much leaves you, with contacts in bigger towns and with access to the house."

"No, I..." Townsend caught the quick movement of Laurenfeld shaking his head. "Just 'no'."

"The other issue is the attack on Officer Reasoner. We know now that it was not done by the same person who," Addams paused on using the particular word, "killed Mrs. Mathison. But there is reason to believe that it was intended to be thought that – that we were supposed to suspect it was done by that same person, as some part of a crazy series of attacks, maybe on lone women. Officer Peabody reported that you were stunned to hear that we had already arrested someone for that first attack and that we knew then that they could not have been done by the same person." Peabody nodded in agreement.

"But nobody else knew it at that time!" Townsend couldn't help saying.

"That is true. But it is a point. That is why we believe the intention was to make it seem like the same attacker."

Addams leaned forward. "You were with Officer Reasoner as you went through the house yesterday and opened the safety deposit box. She may or may not have commented on the smaller size of the room...I suspect she did. It's the sort of thing she would have noticed. But you were aware that she had copied the documents from the bank, including the receipts for adding that extra space to that room. And she would have gone through those papers, finding out about that closet. And that is something you would have wanted to keep hidden."

Addams opened the bag, pulling out the knife and the handkerchief. Townsend's eyes widened as he saw them.

"Do you recognize these, Mr. Townsend?"

"No....Those aren't mine."

Addams noticed the pause. "Do you recognize them?"

"No." This time Townsend shook his head vigorously. "No, I haven't seen them before."

Laurenfeld broke in. "He has answered that question, Chief Addams."

"This knife was used to attack, to stab Officer Reasoner." Addams used the word "stab" deliberately, and Townsend paled slightly at the term. Peabody also grimaced upon hearing the word. "And the handkerchief appears to have been used to wipe the blood off the blade, but not completely enough. They were found in separate trashcans on both the east and west sides of the green. We have warrants to search your residence, your office, and Mrs. Mathison's more specifically for evidence related to both the thefts and the assault on Officer Reasoner.

"You were seen by witnesses afterward at the green, but not until after the ambulance had been called and the rest of the observers had gathered. No one knows where you were prior to or at the time of the attack. You have no alibi, and you could have had time to first attack her, then go to the other side of the green to dispose of the knife, and finally return to join the onlookers."

"I was in the office! I didn't come out till I heard all the noises outside. I didn't hurt Stephanie! I swear!"

Both Addams and Peabody sat back at the vehemence in his voice.

"Mr. Townsend," Laurenfeld interrupted him. "Don't say anything further." He turned to Addams. "Could I have a moment with my client?"

Addams looked at both of them for a moment, then nodded.

"Come on, George. Give them some time." Peabody shut off the recorder, and Addams packed up his evidence into his bag. They went out and shut the door behind them, leaning against the wall outside.

Peabody wiped his forehead.

"My goodness! What do you think?"

"I think...I think we're going to find out what Townsend has to say." Addams smiled slightly. "I also think, that if either of us smoked, this would be the time to do it."

After just a few moments of contemplative silence between the two of them, Matt Laurenfeld opened the door and motioned for them to come back in. They took their seats, and Peabody turned the recorder back on.

Laurenfeld said, "Mr. Townsend would like to make a statement. I want it on record that this is of his own volition, that he is volunteering this information."

Townsend still had his pen in his hand and was now absently clicking it. A nervous habit, but he seemed to need it to keep himself talking.

"I'm not confessing to anything from my old job, but, as you know, we agreed that it was in everyone's best interest for me to look for employment elsewhere. So I came to Summerfield. Aunt Grace knew Mel Johnson, and he was willing to add another man in the office. I think he wants to think about retiring and thought it made sense to have someone take over the business." He looked both Peabody and Addams in the eye. "And I am good at it. I've always had a knack for selling and for getting along with people. So this job really did work for me."

The pen clicked a little more often, and he looked back down at it.

"When I first moved here, Aunt Grace showed me that hidden closet and how to get into it. I, I knew a guy. In Oldstown. A guy that would buy stuff like what you found in there, no questions asked. And I realized that, at garage and yard sales, nobody paid much attention to you. Aunt Grace liked to go to those things, and she would spend time talking to the homeowners. While they were talking, I would wander and found that I could drop a few items in my pockets. At first, just to see if I could get away with it. For the thrill of it. Then I took a few bigger things to the car. Other customers wandering at the sale just think you've already paid for it or are coming back to pay for it. You can carry anything away from a garage sale and, if the owners aren't particularly watching you, no one else thinks anything of it."

He shifted in his seat. Peabody slightly shook his head, but made no comment.

"I'd give Aunt Grace some of the smaller things that didn't seem to have any value – I knew she liked to collect stuff like that. And I told her I had bought some other bigger things and asked if I could keep them in that closet."

Addams interrupted. "Your aunt didn't know these items were stolen?"

Townsend looked up, then back at the table, then at the wall on his right. "No, no, she didn't know."

"She didn't suspect?" Peabody asked.

"If she did, she didn't say anything." He shrugged. "I wasn't going to push it. If she didn't say anything, I certainly wasn't going to."

The clicking pen paused for a moment, then continued.

"So when the closet started to fill up, or I figured it had been long enough since the theft, I'd take whatever we had over to the guy in Oldstown."

He put the pen down and straightened up in his chair.

"So I guess I am confessing to stealing all that stuff in the closet. You got me on that. But I swear to you that I did not attack Officer Reasoner. I may be a thief, but I am not a killer. You were right that she did say something about the room seeming to be much smaller than it should be. But come on, stealing stuff from a yard sale is not going to put me away for life. It's not worth killing somebody over." Townsend spread his hands out on the table. "Hey, come on."

After a moment's silence, Peabody spoke for only the second time, "There is one thing, Mr. Townsend. One of the witnesses said that they saw you throw something into one of the trashcans the night Officer Reasoner was attacked. If it was not the handkerchief, what was it?"

Laurenfeld raised an eyebrow but didn't say anything.

"Oh." Townsend blushed slightly. "I'm kind of, actually very, embarrassed to say this. Especially considering what happened to her. I had gotten Stephanie, Officer Reasoner's phone number from our receptionist and thought that, if she didn't find out about the room, if I wasn't in trouble, I might give her a call sometime about going out to dinner. You know. She is pretty attractive.

"But, after the attack, I thought it might look bad to have a card with her phone number on me. That's what I threw away. Honest."

Peabody rolled his eyes, then stood up and walked down to the end of the room, where Seth Getty had laid out some other items he had found in the trash, not knowing if they would be relevant or not. He sorted through them for a couple of minutes.

"Ah, yeah. Here's an index card with 'SR' and Steph's phone number." He looked back at Townsend. "And three stars?"

Townsend had the grace to grimace. "I always start them out with three stars. But you never know. She could have gotten more."

Addams sighed. "We'll have Marie type this out and then have you sign it, Mr. Townsend. I'm sure District Attorney Alvarez will want to get more detailed in her follow-up interview. Meanwhile, we are going to pursue more information regarding this knife and handkerchief. Thank you for your cooperation."

They all stood. Addams and Laurenfeld shook hands.

"Mr. Laurenfeld, I imagine we'll be seeing a lot of you."

"I suspect so, Chief Addams. DA Alvarez and I will have a lot to discuss."

# CHAPTER 27

As Peabody handed the tape from the recorder to Marie Hazlett, she pointed to two figures sitting in chairs in the department's waiting area. Cecil Skinner and his daughter, Tracy, were waiting patiently, but looked up as Peabody approached.

He shook hands with both of them, making a point of including Tracy. "Thank you for coming, but hold on if you can, for just a minute," he said and walked over to the chief's office. Addams had just sat down.

"The Skinners are here," Peabody announced.

"What? Why?" It took Addams a few seconds to transition from the Townsend interview.

"The girl, Tracy, was one of the witnesses last night, you remember? We had to wait till she got out of school for the day to talk with her?"

"Right, right." Addams nodded in recollection. "Look, could you and... are the Gettys back yet?"

Peabody looked back out at the open room. "No, they're still out doing the searches on Townsend's office and apartment."

"Could you do the interview with her? I need to get my head around some of this earlier stuff. I don't think that she has probably anything new to add, but we do need to get everything in place."

"Yeah, I can handle that."

Peabody grabbed a new tape for his recorder and walked back to the Skinners. "Thanks for coming in. We do really appreciate it. We just want to ask Tracy a few questions about last night, just to make sure we have all the information."

Cecil Skinner looked at his daughter, but she didn't seem to be displaying any signs of being worried about talking with the police. "Okay, that's fine. That's why we're here," he said. "But I want to be with her, to make sure she's okay."

"Sure, no problem. We would want that. We'll meet in Conference Room A right over here." They followed the officer down the hall and into the room.

After they sat down, Peabody remembered he was actually addressing a child and should probably start the interview a little differently. "Tracy, would you like something to drink, a pop or anything?"

Tracy folded her hands on the table. "No, thank you. Dad said we would go out for ice cream after this and I shouldn't have anything else before supper. Mom doesn't want me to have too many sweets."

Peabody tried not to think of the doughnuts that he had eaten so far that day. "Good idea. She's smart, your mom." He took out his notebook, which was filling up. He realized he was going to have to soon get a new one, for the first time in months. He also put a finger over the record button on the tape player and, getting a nod from Tracy's father, pushed it. "First, for the record, I'm going to just ask you some general questions about you, then we're going to go into what you saw last night." Tracy nodded. "Okay, could you tell me your name – your whole name?"

"Tracy Elizabeth Skinner. My middle name is for my great-grandmother. Who I never met."

"Great. I guess I'm named after George Washington, our first president. And how old you are?"

"I'm eleven. But almost twelve. Next month. Dad says I can no longer order off the kid's menu at Mac's Café then, so we better take advantage now."

"And what grade are you in?"

"Sixth grade. I'm in junior high this year."

"Junior high, really? Are you on any of the sports teams? I think that's when they start, isn't it?"

"Well, not the school team. That's seventh grade. But we have a sixth-grade basketball league that plays at the YMCA. I do that, but Jody Spencer hogs the ball and does all the shooting. I don't get to make many baskets. But I have been playing soccer for a couple of years. I'm not very good at it, but I'm getting better."

Peabody laughed. "I think that's really the point at this age – to get better, right?"

Tracy shrugged. "That's what the coach says. And my mom and dad." Like most sixth graders, she probably wanted to be good now, not later.

"Great, you'll get there." Peabody smiled at Cecil Skinner. "Those were the easy questions. Now we're going to get into last night. I understand you were at the village green then, when everything was happening. Can you tell me what you saw?"

"Yes, I was there, but not when the policewoman was hurt. On Wednesdays, I come over to walk Dad home when he gets off work. We sometimes stop for ice cream then too. I like the chocolate pecan, but I'll maybe get peppermint chip if they have it, but they don't always have it. I guess more around Christmastime. But we didn't get any last night because of...you know. That's why we're going this afternoon."

Peabody stifled a chuckle. "Okay. What made you come over to where everybody else was?"

"I heard a loud yell, sort of like 'What?'" Tracy yelled it out. "So I looked over and saw people walking fast toward that little building..."

"The bandstand?"

"Yeah, I guess that's what it's called. So I went over to see what was going on. I was a little early at the grocery store, and Dad wasn't out yet. That lady, Mrs. McMahon, I think her name is, and her dog, Fifi, were also going over. I sometimes get to pet Fifi, so I went over to them."

"Did you see anything?"

"Well, I don't know what you mean by anything."

Peabody nodded in recognition of the vagueness of the question. "I guess I should have just said, what did you see?"

"I saw a lot of people, but it was getting dark out, and I didn't really see anything on the green park area except somebody lying on the ground and a couple of policemen next to them. I guess that was the policewoman." She shrugged. "So I watched the people that were watching, you know what I mean? That's all I could really see. I did see Mr. Peters and that lady from the bank sort of hold hands, but then let go, as if they didn't want anybody to notice that. But I saw them." She giggled. "I know Mr. Peters because he usually has a comic book for me to read when I go into his store with Dad."

"Did you see anybody walk or run away?"

She shook her head. "No. I did see that older man coming from the other side of the park to cross the street, but he was going to where the people that were watching were. He came over and talked with the younger guy, I don't know his name either, coming out of the office right there next to the bank. Well, he's not really young, just not as old."

"Older man? Not Mr. Peters?"

"No, he's taller...and skinnier. Not that Mr. Peters is fat," she looked at her father, but he just raised his eyebrows and didn't say anything. "Just this guy is skinnier. I don't know his name, but I see him downtown sometimes."

"Mr. Johnson? Or Mayor Plummer?"

She shrugged again. "I don't know. Could be, but I don't know which is which. He was somebody I see sometimes, but not so I would know him to talk to. He never says anything to me, except 'Hello, little girl'."

Peabody paused for a moment. "Did you see anybody throw anything away? On the ground, or in the trash can?"

"Yeah, I mean, yes. That lady from the bank, and the one man that came out of the office, and that other guy – the ones I don't know. Right after the second guy crossed the street. They all put something in that trashcan. Oh, and Fifi's owner. She dropped in something that she was carrying." Tracy lowered her voice. "I think it was something Fifi had done. I don't think I'm supposed to say what." She turned to her dad again, but he just smiled and looked the other way.

"You didn't see what any of the rest of them put in there, particularly the men?'

"No, it was all too small. Just something in one hand."

Peabody smiled. "Well, that's more than anyone else could tell me. Thank you. Is there anything else?"

"No, that's when the ambulance came, and then I saw Dad come out of his work, so I said goodbye to Fifi and left."

Peabody stood and leaned over to shake her hand. "I think that's all I need right now, Tracy. Thank you very much. You've been very helpful. We'll let you know if we need anything else." He also shook Mr. Skinner's hand, and the father and daughter left, with Tracy wondering out loud which ice cream she should have on a Thursday.

After they left the building, Peabody went back into the room to sort through the contents of the trashcan again. It didn't take him very long to find what Mrs. McMahon had deposited, and not much more time to discover what Charlene Matthews had probably thrown away.

# CHAPTER 28

Addams entered the conference room just as Peabody was unfolding a piece of paper from the trash. He was followed by both Gettys and Wannamaker, as they had finally returned from their searches.

"You found something?" he asked Peabody.

"Yeah, not really relevant to the attack, but I was following up on what the Skinner girl saw. She said she saw Charlene Matthews throw something into the trash." He held up the paper. "I imagine it was this. It's a note from Hank Peters to her suggesting they meet later that evening. I don't think it's anything we need to pursue." He showed the paper to Addams, who acknowledged it was exactly that, then took it back and put it in his shirt pocket. "But it does seem to confirm their relationship."

Addams raised an eyebrow at his keeping the paper.

"Well, Susan has been wondering about it, as well as half the town. It gives her something that she knows and others don't yet."

Addams rolled his eyes, but didn't say anything. He did go back to the door and call out, "Marie, come in here for a few minutes. We'll leave the door open if the phone rings."

She came in and closed the door behind her. "I *will* know if it rings."

Peabody chuckled. "She always knows. I don't know how, but she always does."

Everybody sat except Addams. Since she didn't expect to be using the board, even Hazlett sat down. He frowned and looked down at the table, then took his seat at the head, in Jeff Pierson's usual seat.

"We need to look at where we are. A lot of things have been happening. Jeff has confessed to Mrs. Mathison's death and is currently in a cell waiting on bail. Harry Townsend has confessed to the thefts of the objects in the hidden closet and is also in a cell. He shouldn't have any trouble making bail for that, but District Attorney Alvarez wants to hold him until we figure out whether we have enough to charge him with the assault on Stephanie. And he steadily denies that assault."

"He is our strongest suspect and the only one with a motive so far, so it is going to be up to us to collect evidence...either to support his guilt or not. What do we have? Sam and Seth, anything from his office or home?"

One of them shook his head, but the other one said, "Well, nothing to tie him in with Officer Reasoner. Nothing that goes with that engraving on the knife, nothing with blood on it. However..."

The first Getty pulled out a list from his notebook. "In his house, we did find three things that matched the reported stolen items. An expensive watch in a drawer, a portable television in his bedroom, and an electric can opener in the kitchen. The television set matched the reported serial numbers, and the watch had engraved initials on the back. Not 'JJ', but 'KC', matching the watch stolen from the Creagers. The can opener had no specific identifying marks, but there was one on the list that was not in the closet, so we're guessing on that one." He folded the paper back up. "That seems to confirm his responsibility for the thefts."

"Anything else?" Addams asked.

This time they both shook their heads.

Wannamaker spoke up. "I found nothing in either of Mayor Plummer's offices or in his home. We drove out there together. I have to tell you, I didn't go into his closets or drawers or anything like that at his home, but I'd rather not unless we have something more to go on. He does have a couple of personal things with 'JJ' on them, like a towel set that has both 'JJ' and 'PJ' for his wife Paula Jean, just things for the bathroom, but there was more with the 'JP' and 'PP' as he had reported. Those were things like personalized stationary or wine glasses or coasters, and it was all something that has both sets of initials, and nothing that looked like that etching on the knife."

Peabody drummed his fingers. "Well, I think we all thought that was a real long shot, didn't we?"

Addams turned to Hazlett. "Marie, you've been on the phone a lot this afternoon. Anything new with you?"

Hazlett didn't need any paper to refer to. "There's no change in

Stephanie's condition. I know we wanted to hear that first.

"The second most important piece of news is that I had Emil Hansfelder and Amos Spencer from Spencer's Antiques go out to Grace Mathison's house to look at the contents of the closet while Phil Culbertson was still there. I wondered about the real value of what was still in the house. Particularly, they looked at the artwork – both paintings and small sculptures, books, and jewelry. Interestingly, some of these are very valuable, real collector's items. In fact, one of the books is a first edition Samuel Clemens. You know, Mark Twain. A first edition Huckleberry Finn, if you can believe it."

"From garage sales?" Peabody interrupted.

Hazlett nodded. "From garage sales. Some of them are listed as stolen, but with no indication that the owners were aware of their worth as anything more than personal possessions."

"You said some of them are listed as stolen?" Addams asked. "So some of them are not?"

"About half of them are on the lists Phil Culbertson had. I plan on looking further back in our records to see if there's anything reported from earlier thefts, maybe even from years before."

"So..." Addams mused, "...and I'm just wondering out loud, is this something that Harry Townsend would have been aware of? That there was a real value to these things? The impression I get is that his crimes were more ones of opportunity than through the expectation of making serious money."

Peabody stirred. "He's already confessed to the thefts."

"I know, I know. I just find it curious. It now magnifies the seriousness of his crimes, which will increase the likelihood of his imprisonment, when he may have thought that he was just looking at probation before. Therefore the confession. But now there's a more vital motive for keeping it secret. And for keeping Stephanie silent."

They all paused for a moment, each in their own thoughts, then Peabody, who hated silences, spoke. "Tracy Skinner turned out to be more observant than all the rest combined. She saw Hank Peters and Charlene Matthews hold hands briefly. No one else in town has ever seen that. She saw three, well, four, people throw something into the trashcan. Mrs.

McMahon threw dog poop – it's over there in a baggie, Mrs. Matthews' note." He held it up. "The 'younger guy', who I assume is Harry Townsend, and an 'older man'. But she doesn't know whether that was Mel Johnson or JJ. She doesn't really know them."

"We do have something we know Townsend threw away," Addams said. Wannamaker and the Gettys looked surprised. Hazlett never seemed surprised by anything. "He said he had a card with Steph's phone number. We found it."

"Was he stalking her?" One of the Gettys asked.

Peabody shook his head. "No, he wasn't, it wasn't anything like that. But don't ask."

The other Getty looked as if he wanted to ask anyway.

Peabody threw his hands up. "He was going to ask her out on a date, okay? It's not a big deal, but I just don't want to think about it."

"That doesn't sound like he was planning on stabbing her," Wannamaker commented.

"No, it doesn't." Peabody didn't appear happy with that conclusion. "But maybe he changed his mind."

Addams continued, getting back to the point he was trying to make, "But we don't know what the 'older man' threw away. There's nothing specific to either JJ or Mel. I looked, but it could have been anything, a tissue, gum, anything."

"Where did the 'older man' come from? And Townsend?" Wannamaker asked.

Peabody pulled out his notebook. "She said she saw Townsend come out of the office, but that doesn't mean he didn't come out earlier and then go back into the office before she got there. The 'older man' came from across the green." He closed the book. "But again that could have been either JJ or Mel. They were both seen coming from that direction."

Addams cocked his head. He looked around the room, but nobody seemed to have anything further to say.

"We have solved two of the three crimes – Mrs. Mathison's death and the yard sale thefts, and we have a suspect already incarcerated for the third – Stephanie's attack. We have direct evidence in the knife and the handkerchief, but have not been able to link them to our suspect. I do have some additional questions now that we know just how valuable some of these stolen objects are, and we are dealing with Townsend's denial of being involved in the attack. His denial made more sense when we thought we were addressing worthless junk, because he didn't have much of a motive, but it also makes sense looking at the fact he had Steph's phone number and apparently hoped to use it. At some point."

He stood up.

"I've got some ideas, but first I need to call District Attorney Alvarez and share with her where we are. Anyone have anything to add?"

There was no response, and he opened the door to leave the room. The others continued to sit, apparently not sure where they would go.

# CHAPTER 29

Martin Addams entered Mac's Café and stopped, his eyes passing over the room. He finally found who he was looking for and walked over to the booth, sliding in on the far side of the table.

"Evening, Mel. Mind if I join you?"

"Bud!" Mel Johnson nodded in surprise. "Go right ahead. Or should I call you 'Chief'?"

"Bud is fine. That's how people know me, and I'd like it to stay that way." Marge MacIntyre placed a glass of water with lemon, and a menu in front of him, but he didn't pick it up. "Give me a couple of minutes, Marge. Don't know how long I'm staying."

Johnson waved at the table. "You're welcome to join me in a meal. I seem to be running out of people to dine with." He sighed. "Grace is dead, Jeff is in jail, I assume Harry is also still in jail." He glanced around the restaurant without really seeing anything, "It's getting lonely."

"I thought you might be interested to know just what is going on now with our investigations. Where we are on the case."

"I certainly would be." Johnson picked up his knife and fork and went back to slicing his broasted chicken. "I appreciate you thinking of me. You must be quite busy."

Addams took a sip of his water. With two lemons, just the way he liked it. Marge never missed a thing.

He lowered his voice so others in the room could not hear and leaned in closer. "As you know by now, Jeff has confessed to killing Grace Mathison, by accident. And then tried to cover it up, by making it look like he hadn't been there. Not the right thing to do of course, but that's what happened. So we're dealing with that now."

Johnson shook his head. "Such a shame all the way around. So senseless." He let out a low breath. "I've heard the stories about it being an accident, and I do know that Jeff would never have done anything to hurt Grace, but what exactly happened?"

"He was at her house to rescue the cat, again. Afterward, as he was inside the house getting dry, he spotted a bowling trophy on her shelf. His bowling trophy, which he didn't know he was missing. He had it in his hand and turned when she came rushing at him, apparently upset for touching her things. The trophy and her head just sort of collided. No intent. No malice, but she was dead." Addams shook his head.

Johnson reached into his pocket but came out with an empty hand, which he put to his mouth and sighed. "No purpose. No reason."

"Then Stephanie was attacked. Since Jeff had just confessed to her and has repeated his confession to us, we knew the attack didn't have anything to do with Mrs. Mathison's death." Addams shrugged. "Could have turned out to be something totally unrelated, but the only thing we had to go on was her part of the investigation into the death, something that she had seen or done or said that was related not to the death, but to the investigation. And the only things she had done differently during those two days was, first, she had been in the house and, second, she had copied some papers from the safety deposit box."

He tapped the table with the spoon, not even realizing he was doing it. "So we started there. In searching the house and from information in the papers that Steph had copied from the bank we found the secret closet with the stolen merchandise from the garage and yard sales. And that led us to Harry Townsend. He has since confessed to the thefts, but continues to deny stabbing Stephanie. In fact, he said he had a note with her phone number on it, intending to call her later. We have found that note."

"He was going to call her? About what?" Johnson barely breathed.

Addams paused for a moment. "Apparently he liked her. You'll have to take that up with him. It's just an indication that he had planned to talk with her later, which is inconsistent with trying to kill her sooner.

"And we think we have found the knife used in the assault, in a trashcan on the far side of the green. And a handkerchief possibly used to wipe the knife in a different trashcan." Johnson had been wiping his mouth with a napkin, but he quickly put it down. "Two different trashcans, on two different sides of the green.

"At this point, we have not been able to tie either of them directly to Harry Townsend. He is our primary suspect, but the theft of minor objects that people were looking to get rid of anyway doesn't seem enough of a motive for an attempted murder. Does it?"

"Then surely Office Reasoner's attack can have nothing to do with the thefts," Johnson said. He appeared to have forgotten his meal. "It must have been something else. I can assure you Harry would have had nothing to do with trying to hurt her. Was there another case she was working on? Maybe something in her personal life, an old boyfriend?" There was a hopeful note in his voice.

"It does seem to be that we were supposed to think it was something else. I believe that originally we were supposed to suspect it was the same person that attacked Grace." Johnson nodded at that. "But the person who stabbed Stephanie didn't know that we had already found that...had already got Jeff for that. No one did. Actually no one outside of Stephanie herself, but since Jeff confessed again immediately, it certainly was not an attempt to silence her."

Addams took another sip of water. He appeared to stare over Johnson's right shoulder while thinking of what to say next. But he actually was looking at a booth across the room. George Peabody and the Skinner family were sitting in that booth, with Peabody and Tracy facing Addams. Peabody turned to Tracy. She nodded, and he passed the nod on to Addams.

He continued in a low voice, tapping his spoon even more quickly. "It still could have been for something else, but then we found the knife and handkerchief. And Marie discovered something else, something that may have changed the motive. There weren't just knick-knacks and worthless throwaways in that closet. Some of them were really very valuable. The jewelry and the books and the artwork. She called some of the owners. They had no idea any of it was worth anything. Some of the stuff had never even been reported as stolen. But somebody knew the value. And the crime scene team found quite a few tea boxes full of cash in Grace Mathison's kitchen – over thirty-six thousand dollars. That's a lot of money from clipping coupons. I think Grace not only knew about the stolen merchandise but knew it was valuable stuff."

Addams shook his head. "But I still don't see her actually stealing the bigger items or knowing where to sell it. She seemed to be a collector, but only of small things, the things she could tell stories about."

Johnson put down his fork, but he hadn't really eaten anything for a while. "Grace liked her stories. The only value her possessions had was for prompting those stories."

"We have a witness." Addams took a deep breath. "Not of the attack, but a witness who saw several people throw things into the trashcan. And who saw someone come from across the green, from where the can with the knife was."

"Well, I assume several people could have thrown stuff away. That doesn't mean anything."

Addams nodded. "As a matter of fact, the witness did see four people throw things in that can. We have discovered all four, three of them consistent with what they said."

Johnson picked up his check and started to move out of the booth. "I really hate to do this, but I have an appointment, Bud. I really want to hear what you have to say, but I'm running late as it is. Maybe we can meet tomorrow?"

He stood up, appeared to notice George Peabody in the other booth for the first time, and Addams saw him also take note of two young men at the table closest to the door. No food in front of them. Marge and Cathy, the other waitress, were still waiting on tables, but "Mac" MacIntyre and Mike Wannamaker were standing near the door to the kitchen. The men were all looking at him. Johnson put down the check and sat back down. He started to reach into a coat pocket, but stopped halfway and picked up the napkin to wipe his brow.

"The witness saw you coming back from the other side of the green, Mel, and toss something into the trashcan." Addams breathed out, "Mel, what did you throw away?"

"I... I don't remember."

Addams nodded as if he expected that response.

"You're in the insurance business, Mel. Have been for years. You insure for life, death, home, personal possessions...pretty much everything, right, Mel?"

Mel gave a quick nod. He picked up the napkin again and started to fold and refold it.

"And you know the value of the personal possessions. Or at least know how to find out the value. And you might be the one to know where those types of possessions might be sold. That was one of the problems with both Harry and Grace. That knowledge. Harry has been with you for a little while now and has probably picked up a few things. But the records show that room was put in a long time before Harry came to town, and it turns out that many of the more valuable items in that closet? Many of them were stolen before he was here too."

Addams shifted in his seat. Johnson just looked down at the table.

"Steph went through the house and the safety deposit box with Harry Townsend. But they weren't the only ones there. You were there also. You heard her say something about the size of that room."

"She said she wanted to come back and measure it." Johnson spoke in a low voice, still looking at the table.

"And you saw her take those documents from the safety deposit box. Once she looked through those papers, she would know why the room was smaller. And when that closet was added.

"I notice you seem to be missing your handkerchief, Mel. It is well known that you prefer to carry a handkerchief to a tissue. I'm surprised you didn't replace it, but I guess it was just habit not to do it yet. Or you just hadn't gotten around to it, since the attack was only last night. We got a warrant to search your residence this afternoon, just within the past two hours as a matter of fact. We found a few other items with that stylized 'JJ' that was on the knife -- a pen set with personalized correspondence paper and a set of linen napkins. Your company name, Johnson and Johnson, wasn't just to sound impressive. When you started, it was with your father. He was the original Johnson and you were added later. If we go to your office, we'll probably find a few more things with those initials. We just haven't gotten there yet."

Addams stopped talking. After a few moments, Johnson looked up, but he appeared to have aged ten years.

He looked at the closer tables before speaking slowly, haltingly, and little more than above a whisper. Addams had to cock his head to make sure he heard all the words. "Several years ago, well, more than a few anyway, Ralph Mathison and I went to a yard sale with our wives. I think it was the Hufnagels' sale, people who bought what they liked but with no sense of style or value. They had their insurance through me, and, once I saw what they were selling, I realized they had no idea what anything was worth. There were a couple of pieces of jewelry and a painting. I'm no art expert, but it looked like an original SanGennaro. You may or may not know that those are worth something. I bought the painting for about ten bucks – I think they were really selling the frame, and I slipped a piece of the jewelry into my pocket. Just did it without really thinking about it. I had it in my hand and turned to look at something else. Ralph saw me do that, looked around, then he took a bracelet and put it in his pocket. Then he grinned as if he was getting away with something. Well, we both got away with something. I had sold some things I inherited from a great-aunt to this second-hand place in Oldstown. I don't think he regards himself as a fence, he just doesn't ask any questions. So I took those pieces to him, both the art and the necklace, and Ralph's bracelet. He gave me three thousand dollars for them, two thousand for the painting and five hundred each for the jewelry. On an investment of ten dollars.

"There were more sales the next weekend. I had policies on several of those families. I checked them and realized there were no significant valuables listed, just the home and general contents. But one of the sales had three rare books and a small antique end table that should definitely have been insured."

"Why didn't you just pay the low price for them?"

Marge started to approach the table, but Peabody called her before she got too close and she went over to where he was sitting.

Both the men had stopped talking briefly while she was near. Johnson grimaced and squirmed in his seat. "Looking back, we should have. At the time, it was sort of exciting. We discovered that if we didn't actually buy anything, nobody remembered us being there at all. Grace would usually talk with the owners to keep them busy, my wife never knew any of this. If somebody did start talking with us, then we'd buy something small or pay the marked price. If nobody did, we just walked off. If anyone else at the sale saw us, they just assumed we had already paid for it. We also didn't want to get a reputation for underpaying for an item, then making a fortune reselling it and somebody might ask us later what we had done with that old painting of Aunt Martha's." He shrugged. "It was just easier not to pay for it in the first place. And nobody seemed to really care." Johnson sort of half-smiled. "And we were getting kind of a rush out of it, kind of a thrill, a shock of adrenalin. Even if something was reported as stolen, as not accounted for in their sales, there was never much of an investigation because they simply weren't regarded as being worth much. I only had one or two insurance claims and then only for very small amounts."

"What about all the knick-knacks?"

"Ralph got those as gifts for Grace. He'd just pick up miscellaneous boxes. I think she realized he might not have paid for all of them, but that just added to the mystery for her, made the stories more exciting – as if they were part of a secret treasure."

"And when did the spare room come into being?"

"At first we just put them in the Mathison garage, but that was too visible, and Grace wouldn't have accepted us having those out in plain sight. So Ralph had the secret closet added. Grace never went in that room.

"And Ralph was the one that first used the tea boxes to store the cash. He never really did it for the money. It was the excitement of not getting caught. We both figured no one was getting hurt – they were just getting rid of these things as junk anyway. The money was for Grace after he died, but I don't think she ever counted it. Maybe took out a twenty every once in a while. I kept putting her share in there, but I don't think she even noticed."

Johnson took a sip from his water glass. He had been talking for some time, as if he had been feeling the need to tell somebody. Finally.

When he spoke again, his voice was a little bit stronger. "After Ralph died, we stopped doing anything for a while. But then Harry had to leave his job and came to Summerfield. I knew why he left, and it seemed natural to use him for the lawn sales. He seemed to get a kick out of it."

Addams stirred and wished he had gotten something stronger to drink. Maybe with three or four lemons.

"So why the attack on Stephanie? As Harry said, what you stole didn't seem worth it."

"Over the years there was quite a bit more money than Harry knew about. We'd have gotten in serious trouble for taxes over it." Johnson grimaced. "I'll get in trouble over the taxes. It's a bigger deal than the petty larceny that Harry figures it is."

He looked into space for a moment, then sighed deeply. With years of regret behind it.

"And there's my reputation in this town. I'm considered somebody here. Somebody of importance." He brought his eyes back to Addams' face. "You're right. I heard Stephanie say she was going to come back and measure the room. I saw her make copies of the documents at the bank. I knew she was wondering what the heck Grace was doing with so much money. In tea boxes, for Christ's sake. She was going to find the room, and it was going to come back to me, and everyone in town was going to know I was a thief." His voice had been getting louder, but Johnson started and looked around quickly. Nobody nearby appeared to be paying attention.

He resumed speaking more quietly. "I've been here too long, I've done too much. The knife is something I carry out of habit when I go home and when I come to work in the morning. I don't really know why, my father gave it to me when I first started here, and I carry it in case I'm carrying money, but I've never even taken it out before. I keep it in a sheath that hooks down inside of my pants. Nobody else even knew I had it. That night, as I left the office, I just happened to see Stephanie come around the corner of the bandstand and no one else was out on the sidewalks yet. I just did it." He held his hands up. "I just...did it."

He looked at his hands hanging in the air as if he couldn't believe what they had done. Addams didn't say anything. Johnson clenched his hands into fists and slowly lowered them to the table.

"It was an impulse – without really thinking. Just like taking the yard sale stuff in the first place." He gave a harsh laugh. "Only two really impulsive things I've done in my life." He shifted in his seat. "I guess I thought people would just assume it was the same person that had killed Grace. I knew that wasn't Harry or me, so I figured no suspicion would fall on us. I had no way of knowing that case was already solved. I ran across to the other side of the green and got rid of the knife as soon as I could, just to get it out of my hands. I wiped it with my handkerchief, the only thing I had, but I saw people gathering and thought I should hurry back and act like I had just come out of my office. But nobody paid any real attention to me, and I finished wiping any blood off my hands and just dropped the handkerchief into that other trashcan, the one closer to the office. I wanted to get that blood away from me."

Both of them just looked down at the table for several minutes.

"So this," Addams finally spoke again. "All of this – the covering up of Mrs. Mathison's death, the attack on Stephanie – has been about reputation, keeping the good name that had been established in this town. Jeff didn't want the townsfolk to think of him as a police chief who accidentally killed people, and you didn't want them realizing you were stealing from them. That you were actually taking advantage of the people that were looking up to you."

Addams sat for a few minutes more, then waved for Peabody to come over. Peabody finished chewing his last bite of chocolate pecan pie then reluctantly pushed the rest of it in front of Tracy. He stood and walked over to the table. The Gettys stood but stayed where they were, in front of the door.

"George, we're going to arrest Mr. Johnson here on the same charge for theft that we used for Harry Townsend this afternoon. And for the charge of assault, attempted murder, of Stephanie Reasoner. This time, we're going to use both charges.

Peabody gently pulled Johnson to his feet and started reading him his rights. Johnson didn't resist as the handcuffs were put on and nodded in understanding of his rights, but then turned to Addams. He turned so that the handcuffs were not obvious to the other customers.

"Bud, I want you to know that at some point I would have confessed to everything. It all got out of control so quickly. Everything went to crap. Tell me, what's going on with Officer Reasoner?" He looked Addams straight in the eyes with apparent sincere concern. "I really regret that, truly."

"We got word just before I came over that she was now out of critical condition and had recovered consciousness, but was not yet ready to speak. She is going to survive. It's going to be a long haul, but she is going to survive."

"I'm glad of that." He took a deep breath and slowly let it out. "I am sorry. I... I don't know what else to say." Glancing down, he noticed his dinner. "Considering everything, I hate to ask this, but could you take care of the bill for me? I can't seem to get to my money right now."

Addams looked at the barely-touched meal, then ruefully smiled and took out his wallet.

"Oh, what the hell. I'm supposed to be getting a raise being Chief, I hope."

# CHAPTER 30

Martin Addams took advantage of the fact that the other two cells were momentarily unoccupied and opened the door to Jeff Pierson's cell. Not even bothering to shut the door, he sat down on the edge of the bed facing Pierson who had been reading at the one desk.

"Bud." Pierson set his book face down. "Do I need my lawyer here with me?"

"No." Addams shook his head. "No, Jeff. I just wanted to talk. Mel's with your lawyer – his lawyer – Harry's lawyer. And Harry is taking a shower. I just wanted some time with just the two of us." He stretched his neck in weariness. "This has been a hell of a few days." He laughed softly. "Just three days. Can you believe it?"

Pierson inclined his head. "You wrapped up three cases in just three days. That's pretty quick. I never did anything like that. Certainly not three cases with three perpetrators, all needing to be locked up."

"I didn't do it all. Steph found you." Addams looked him in the eye. "It all started with an accident."

Pierson looked at the wall and drummed his fingers on the desk. "It, it just happened, Bud. It just happened." He sighed. "And then I went stupid."

"And then you went, as you say, stupid. And that's what's true for most of what happened. Only Harry's crime – theft – was typical, and it's going to be the least of them. Both you and Mel got in much more trouble for trying to cover up, for trying to protect your reputations."

Pierson spoke low, still looking away. "I did it, Bud, I killed Grace Mathison. I admit it. I'm not trying to explain away anything. I know I should have just called for the squad right away. There's no real justification for it." He turned back to Addams. "But you have to understand, Bud. It was stupid, but all that I could think of at the time was that this is my town.

These are my people. They have to trust me, they have to believe that I would never do anything to hurt them. My whole career has been for nothing if they can't, if they couldn't do that." He went back to facing the wall. "But that's all gone anyway."

Addams looked down at the floor. "That's the same sort of thing that Mel Johnson said. That it was important what people thought of him. The difference is that Mel betrayed them in the first place, then attacked Stephanie to keep them from finding out. You tried to cover up a mistake. There was no malice in your actions." He straightened up. "But Jeff, I think you underestimated your people. They would have been upset by what happened, sure. They may have been dismayed, they may have tried to rationalize that you could have done something different, that you could have put the trophy down before turning around. But they would have recognized it as an accident. They wouldn't have feared you. They would still have believed in you as the police chief. You would have gotten past it. And you'll still get past this. You're not in the deepest trouble for her death, but more for trying to cover it up. There will be consequences. I'm not kidding you, serious consequences, you know that. For her death, but not as a murder, as an accident. Summerfield will still believe in you as a person. You and your family have to know that."

Pierson slowly nodded. "Thank you, Bud, I do appreciate it. I think it's going to take a while before I believe it, though."

Addams stood up. "Everybody knows everyone in this town. Everyone is family. Some things you can forgive in family, some things you can't. Mel and Harry betrayed their confidence and continue to betray it. You didn't. You're going to be okay. I believe that."

They shook hands, and Addams walked out of the cell, slowly, reluctantly shutting the door behind him.

# CHAPTER 31

Judy Pierson took a deep shuddering breath and walked through the front doors into The Southern Westside Memorial Hospital. She kept her head down, not knowing who she might see in the lobby, or worse, who might see her. It had only been a couple of weeks since the storm and its aftermath – Mrs. Mathison's death and the following events. The town would never be the same, would never completely trust in each other, and she didn't know how much of a target of that distrust that she might become.

The receptionist wasn't familiar to her and didn't respond except to give her the room number she wanted. She hurried to the elevator and was glad that no one else got on with her. She finished the ride trying to think of what she might say. Everything she had practiced on the drive here still didn't sound right. There was going to be blame and tears and guilt. But she still had to make this visit. It was important.

Once she was at the door, it took three deep breaths before she pushed it open and stepped inside.

To find the room full. Instead of just the one person that she had been fearing facing, there were four women. And they all turned to stare at her as she came in.

Stephanie Reasoner looked up from her bed. "Judy! Oh, my God! I am so glad to see you!"

Marie Hazlett was the first one to come to her, holding her arms out for a hug. "Judy, why didn't you tell me you were coming? We'd have given you a ride."

Judy returned the hug, tentatively at first, then stronger as she was reassured by the fierceness of Marie's hold. When Marie finally released her, Susan Peabody stepped in her for her turn, giving a hug just as strong, just as meaningful.

"I…" Judy was holding back tears already. "I wasn't expecting anyone else here. I just thought I should come to see, to see how Steph is doing."

From her left, Sherri Northrup stood up from her seat and gave her the brief hug of acquaintances. "Hey, Mrs. Pierson. I guess we all had the same idea. You know what they say, great minds, huh?" She stepped back and let Judy move up to the head of the bed.

"Oh, Steph," she hesitantly started to say, but couldn't continue when Stephanie held out her arms, and they both started crying. They held each other for what seemed like long moments but was not long enough.

Judy straightened up. "I don't want to hurt you. I don't know how sore you are, or what you can do?" It ended up as a question.

Stephanie smiled. "I'm fine." She shrugged. "Well, considering, I guess I'm okay. Hugs are therapeutic anyway."

Judy looked at the other women, then back at Stephanie. She wiped her tears with the back of her hand. Susan offered her a tissue. "I, I don't know what to say. I practiced coming over here, but…I just wanted to see you."

"You're here. That's all you need to say. I am so glad to see you."

Everybody started to cry again, even Marie, almost.

"Sit down, Mrs. Pierson, sit down." Sherri indicated the chair that she had been in. "I need to leave soon anyway."

"Are you sure, Sherri?" Judy took the seat. "Thank you. I appreciate it."

"Sure. My shift is going to start soon." She glanced at her watch. "Since the insurance office closed, I'm now at the receptionist's desk downstairs. You probably passed Lisha as you came in. She's going to say that she got me this job, but she just happened to know that there was an opening because they were trying to get her to work more."

"Oh, Sherri." Judy put out her hand to the younger woman's arm. "I am so sorry about your job."

"Hey, you didn't have anything to do with it. Besides, it worked out better. I'm actually making a little more money. But…" Sherri leaned toward her and grinned. "And this is actually the big part, I'm able to talk with more people. All day long. And they're happy to spend time talking with me. At Johnson and Johnson, they usually were complaining about something – something they wanted to add or a claim they needed to file. But here, they really seem to enjoy just talking, and having me talk with them. I love it."

She touched Judy on the shoulder. "Look, it's good to see you, but I do have to go. You have a nice visit and be sure to stop at the front desk when you come back." She waved at the others and left.

Susan sat down in the other chair. It was assumed by everybody, and rightly so, that Marie would prefer to stand. They all looked at Judy, and Stephanie asked the question.

"How are you? Really. And... how is Jeff? We've been so worried about him."

"You've been worried...about Jeff? After everything that happened, and after what happened to you?"

Stephanie nodded. "Yes, I am. He didn't have anything to do with this. I'm going to live. I'll be back on my feet."

"Of course we're concerned, Judy." Susan added. "About Jeff and you. We care – we're all one family. That's the way we work."

Judy put her hand to her mouth. "I'm, I'm okay. Everyone has been nice to me. The neighbors have brought over food, but I think that's just as much to see what's going on. Pastor Johns stops in every couple of days, and he and Jeff have a good talk. Jeff is, well he doesn't want to get out much. He's out on bail, you probably know."

Marie nodded. "I told them."

"I think Matt Laurenfeld is trying to work out some sort of deal for Jeff...and for all of them. Everybody knows what they did, so there's not much point in going to trial. Nobody's denying anything anymore."

"I think that would be best," Marie said, but then she looked at Stephanie. She nodded in agreement. "Yes, I agree. Let's get this done and move on."

Judy asked, to change the subject, "Steph, how much longer are you going to be here?"

"Just a few more days, I think. When the therapists are sure I'm going to be steady enough to not fall and hurt myself again." She laughed. "Well, pretty sure anyway. I could still fall, just for the heck of it." She pointed at the other two. "Marie and Susan, and Sherri as a matter of fact, have worked out a schedule to watch over me, I mean, help me around the house as they put it."

Marie smiled slightly, as much as she ever smiled. "We need her back.

George is trying to train the Gettys, but I think he's, what they call micro-managing, rechecking everything they do."

It was Susan's turn to laugh. "Yeah, probably, but he loves it. I think it makes him feel young and useful again. He's even getting friskier at home."

"And," Marie continued. "We've got that extra desk waiting for you, Steph. Well, actually it's the same old desk that you had, but no one is using it. And you better get back before it becomes the file table, or the snack table, or whatever George decides to use it for."

Stephanie shook her head. "It's going to be a little while yet. And I think Bud's got a handle on it. I think you're in good hands right now."

"Oh, we need you, don't think we don't." Marie cocked her head. "Bud has grown up a lot in the past few weeks. I have to give him credit for that. But I do think he would really like your experience and knowledge by his side. You're the one that really had this all figured out – Jeff, the size of the room, the extra money in the house. We need you back."

They sat in silence for a moment. But, to Judy, it was the most comfortable silence she had experienced in several weeks. She was with friends, and they were still friends. They accepted her. They still accepted her as one of them, as one of their family. There were issues yet to be resolved, but, for the first time in a while, she felt she might be able to get past them.

"Judy?" Susan broke the silence. "Judy, you read a lot, don't you? I think you might like to sit in on my book club. Actually, we don't always talk about books, but it's fun, it's good to get together."

Judy smiled. She liked books. She could do that.

# ABOUT THE AUTHOR

Kevin Creager is a school psychologist who has previously published *We Cuss a Little: The Life and Times of a School Psychologist*, named one of the nine essential books for a school psychologist. He grew up in a small town where everyone knew everyone else. His wife and three grown children work hard to keep him in touch with the real world.

Thank you so much for reading one of our **Crime Fiction** novels.
If you enjoyed our book, please check out our recommended title for your
next great read!

*Bailey's Law* by Meg Lelvis

"An intelligent, immersive police procedural that will leave you pining for
another Jack Bailey novel." *—BEST THRILLERS*

View other Black Rose Writing titles at www.blackrosewriting.com/books

and use promo code **PRINT** to receive a **20% discount** when purchasing.